WHAT GOES AROUND

a novel by

Ruth Clarke

INANNA PUBLICATIONS AND EDUCATION INC.
TORONTO, CANADA

Copyright © 2019 Ruth Clark

Except for the use of short passages for review purposes, no part of this book may be reproduced, in part or in whole, or transmitted in any form or by any means, electronically or mechanically, including photocopying, recording, or any information or storage retrieval system, without prior permission in writing from the publisher or a licence from the Canadian Copyright Collective Agency (Access Copyright).

Canada Council for the Arts   Conseil des Arts du Canada

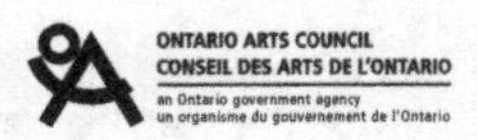

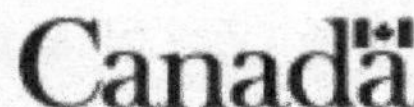

We gratefully acknowledge the support of the Canada Council for the Arts and the Ontario Arts Council for our publishing program. We also acknowledge the financial support of the Government of Canada.

Cover design: Val Fullard

What Goes Around is a work of fiction. All the characters portrayed in this book are fictitious and any resemblance to persons living or dead, is purely coincidental.

Library and Archives Canada Cataloguing in Publication

Title: What goes around : a novel / Ruth Clarke.
Names: Clarke, Ruth, 1950– author.
Series: Inanna poetry & fiction series.
Description: Series statement: Inanna poetry & fiction series
Identifiers: Canadiana (print) 20190147776 | Canadiana (ebook) 20190147784 | ISBN 9781771336574 (softcover) | ISBN 9781771336581 (epub) | ISBN 9781771336598 (Kindle) | ISBN 9781771336604 (pdf)
Classification: LCC PS8605.L3668 W53 2019 | DDC C813/.6—dc23

Printed and bound in Canada

Inanna Publications and Education Inc.
210 Founders College, York University
4700 Keele Street, Toronto, Ontario, Canada M3J 1P3
Telephone: (416) 736-5356 Fax: (416) 736-5765
Email: inanna.publications@inanna.ca Website: www.inanna.ca

To the memory of the fine storyteller,
Max Johnson,
who owned the bird.

1.

THE FIRST TIME I FLEW to Guanacaste province in Costa Rica was in the seventies and it was with my bride. The Cessna we'd taken from the airport in Alajuela had landed in a dusty field. It was cowboy country then, where *vaqueros* cantered by on sandy streets, digging their spurs into plump glossy steeds whose necks arched dramatically while they pranced and kicked up dust as they passed by. This time I was alone, divorced from my second wife, and the plane was a Boeing 737 that landed at a new airport in Liberia, serving passengers with Pacific coast destinations.

It was early November; the rainy season was drawing to a close. The last time I was here was in January, and the vegetation had been green and healthy, but now the foliage was boisterously lush, the rivers swollen; I swear you could see things grow. The landscape had evolved with the passage of time; development loomed large and buildings dotted the horizon with architectural palaces built into the mountains, affording the best views. But where I was going, it was like stepping back in time.

My Spanish had improved marginally since the seventies, but I still wasn't fluent; however, my real estate agent spoke some English, so with our combined efforts we were able to understand each other. When I had decided to make the move, I'd found his name on a website, and we'd communicated over the past few months. He knew my budget, that

I wanted shoreline, a fairly good-sized house and property. He met me at the airport and took me to a farm that he admitted he had only driven by, but assured me it met all of my requirements. It was one of the original haciendas, more than one hundred years old, with shoreline near Playa Tamarindo. He was selling it for an elderly couple who were too old to worry about it, anxious to sell after the occupants had deserted. Though I kept my mouth shut, I thought the price was ridiculously low.

When we entered the house, it appeared that the occupants had indeed left in a hurry. Inside the old frame building, the still life arrangement we saw was like a diorama depicting rural Costa Rican life. Coffee ringed the cups in rusty stains; curled and dried-up tortillas with teeth marks in them rested against *gallo pinto,* the ubiquitous Tico breakfast of rice and beans, now dried like black-and-white pebbles. In the guestroom, everything was in order: an embroidered bedspread covered the mattress, lace curtains framed a view of the orchard, and bright, cheerful, naïve paintings hung on the walls. But in the master bedroom, men's and women's clothes—dresses, jeans and underwear—were strewn everywhere. The bed was unmade, and I sensed what had been a desperate departure. Running from what, I wondered?

When I said I would take it, the agent drove me to his office in Tamarindo, where I signed the papers. I gave him ten thousand dollars in cash, wrote a cheque for the balance of sixty thousand, and pocketed the receipt that I would exchange for the deed when my cheque cleared, which would probably be within a month or so. But I was able to move in on the strength of my deposit. The agent seemed to know everyone in the area and told me about a 2001 Toyota Corolla that was for sale—a "beater," as we would call it where I come from—but it ran and that was all I needed. And he offered to send a woman to clean the place.

Unlike the real estate agent, Maria spoke not a word of

English. When he dropped her off, he had explained what needed to be done, and she and I were left to our mutual form of communication: body language. She worked hard setting the house back in order while I explored the outbuildings.

A rusted iron pump handle stood on a platform over a disused well. It must have been a perch of choice, for a substantial pile of bird droppings skirted the area below the handle. A shed next to the house contained ancient tools, shovels, rakes, and earthen pots that were chipped and cracked. From the dried balls of manure in the barn and the size of the stalls, it looked like horses had been kept there, maybe ridden away by the fleeing occupants. Chickens pecked listlessly at the ground outside the barn and became enthused and vocal when I found a bag of corn to scatter for them.

When I returned to the house, the transformation was miraculous. The table had been cleared and reflected a lustrous glow. The tile floors had returned to their original creamy background with cross-hatches of mint green and cranberry glazes. Low afternoon light shone through sparkling windows edged in crisp eyelet curtains that appeared freshly laundered. Fresh linens covered the bed in the master bedroom; the soiled linens, now washed, hung like benign amorphous ghosts over the bushes outside. Maria had emptied the closets of the previous owners' clothing, filling several bulging garbage bags. I motioned and tried to tell her that if she knew of anyone who could use the clothes, she was welcome to take them. I think she understood for she lugged the bags to the door and left them there.

On a pedestal in the corner of the living room stood a large birdcage, its door still open, though the seeds, droppings, and feathers I'd seen on the floor when I first arrived were gone. Maria came into the room while I was standing there, and we both raised our eyebrows and shrugged. I wondered if the bird had fled with the occupants. I smiled, imagining the bird clutching one of the riders on the galloping horses, perhaps flying for a distance, then returning to rest again. But I didn't know enough Spanish to share my fantasy.

I paid her and lamely attempted to ask her if she would come again in two weeks, pointing to a date on the calendar on the fridge, then to her, motioning around the house. She nodded and smiled, and I grinned, hopefully indicating my satisfaction. I drove her home that day, carried the bulky bags through her stiflingly hot little bungalow onto a little patio that served as a laundry room.

The grounds around my house were void of lawns, save the odd clump of escaped beach grass waving triumphantly. Paths of oyster shells meandered to the barn, around to the shed, and into the orchard of flourishing fruit trees. I spent the rest of the afternoon picking oranges, lemons, and mangoes from the orchard and a ripe watermelon from a sprawling vine near the house. I'd bought a few groceries in town, and after harvesting what I could from the orchard, I settled in a rocking chair on the veranda with a cold beer to watch the sunset. I could hear the surf pounding beyond the dune that acted as a barrier to the offshore winds. When I'd finished my beer, I kicked off my shoes and walked down to the beach. It was my beach now, though all owners of shoreline had to observe the fifty-metre zone. The first fifty metres above the median high tide was considered public lands, and therefore, protected. To the north of me was the Tamarindo estuary, part of the Parque Nacional Marino Las Baulas. *Baulas* are sea turtles. The leatherback turtles come up on shore to lay their eggs on the beaches around here at the end of the rainy season, and the fifty-metre zone would presumably protect their nests. It was a good law, in my estimation.

I walked around the clumps of tall grasses that anchored the sand on the dune, valuable plants in the prevention or lessening of erosion from incessant offshore winds. Pleasant and refreshing, but they could change the landscape in a matter of hours.

The silhouette of a freighter heading north caught the bleeding edge of the setting sun; three shrimp trawlers plied the waters half a mile out. And suddenly, a large lime green dart flashed past me, a lone bird headed for one of the fruit trees, perhaps. At the shoreline, I walked in the cool waters of the incoming tide, my footprints ephemeral markings that quickly disappeared, leaving no trace. Then the windswept silence was suddenly shattered by a desperate cry—someone in pain or distress—that ceased in an instant. I dismissed what I'd heard, blamed it on the wind rustling through the dune grass or the bamboo rattling near my house.

I walked back and started the propane stove to cook a breast of chicken and while it simmered I returned to the veranda and listened to a choir of crickets whose song reverberated in the night air. I made a salad and brought my dinner out to the table, dining beneath a twinkling chandelier of stars. Once again, in the twilight, I caught a glimpse of the bright green parrot, this time, landing on the pump handle.

Over the next few days, I rummaged around in the shed and found a hammer and some nails, and with some poles I'd found in the barn, I fashioned a makeshift easel on my veranda, which had become my living and dining rooms and would now become my studio. I started painting again, albeit with some trepidation, fearful that my confidence and skill had atrophied during my divorce from Ingrid little more than a year ago.

My work was anomalous in the New York scene of dramatic installations, loud or cerebral or angry statements against society. Yet, amid that city of imposing concrete canyons that hurled the biting cold winter winds down its corridors, and in summer held the oppressive humidity captive, I had, with my canvases, created a tropical oasis, a haven, which had drawn an audience. Young couples, old spinsters, middle-aged corporate lawyers, and bankers, all attended my exhibitions and purchased my work. And none of them had worn Tilley hats. One critic had described my work as "bold, vibrant celebrations of nature." My "reverence for nature" had taken me around the globe; it had drawn me to Costa Rica, to this living gallery of the senses.

My first attempt was of the landscape in front of me—the dune and the ocean dotted with fishing and sailboats. I felt like a student again; as I brushed the sheet, I heard disparaging comments from my instructor, admonishing my elementary talents, my fear of meeting the challenge. I burned that sheet in the *chimenea*, the finest editor an artist can ever have.

But the following day, when I stapled the next sheet on the easel, I sensed confidence in my brush strokes: bold, compelling, and thankfully familiar. Overnight, the muscle had toned; or had I dreamed confidence? Anyway, I was ready. My subject was the parrot, a regular visitor to the pump handle, the growing mounds beneath it attesting to the regularity of its bowels and the frequency of his visits. I was convinced that the cage belonged to my visitor, though it appeared to be enjoying its freedom, so I didn't try to coax it into the house.

The days passed quickly. There always seemed to be something to do. First, the prerequisite early morning walk on the beach to see what had rolled in on the waves—interesting shells, driftwood, and tumbled pieces of coloured glass to add to my growing beachcombing collection. Then I would return to make coffee, sit on the veranda, and summon the muse. Painting, harvesting, pruning trees, feeding the chickens, shopping, and generally trying to keep the place in some semblance of order until Maria arrived to set it right, took up my waking hours. I tumbled into bed early each night, and my sleep was glorious, deep, and uninterrupted.

When Maria arrived again, I was at my easel. She seemed curious; perhaps she'd never seen an artist at work. I beckoned for her to take a look. My subject was on his rusted pump handle and she nodded, pointing, acknowledging the likeness. She went about her work, humming and singing to the radio I'd tuned to a local station. When she started scrubbing the floor, the tap water trickled to a halt so she carried her pail out to the pump to collect water. As she approached the pump, I recognized the cries I'd heard the other night; they were coming from the parrot, followed by a stream of incomprehensible Spanish, which sounded relaxed and chatty, then, somewhat hysterical. Maria appeared startled by what she heard and even crossed herself. The parrot flew to a nearby mango tree and continued screaming. Maria looked at me with a worried expression, fear in her eyes. I shrugged, not understanding what the parrot was saying, not knowing what to say to placate Maria, nor how to say it. She managed to pump enough water to finish the floors, and the parrot remained in the trees, finally quiet.

I bought a Spanish-English dictionary and started to look up words that I needed to be able to communicate with Maria. I'd asked her to come once a week now, since I was becoming more involved in my painting and outside chores. By the time she arrived the following week, I was able to ask her what the parrot was saying, though I couldn't understand her response and asked her to write it down for me.

When I looked up the words in my dictionary, I was surprised, to say the least. The parrot was saying, "Long trip. Home again. Please don't hit me. Don't hit me." This stream of words would be followed by obvious crying sounds—*that* I could understand. Now, when the parrot arrived at his perch, I recognized the Spanish words. Some sounded mature and confident; other expressions sounded concerned, even terrified. The parrot recited his litany of expressions without emotion, insensitive to the fearful human cries that he had doubtless heard more than once.

Maria had been coming to the house for a month when, once again, there was no tap water. She carried her pail to the pump, but when she had drawn only a fraction of the pail, she yelled for me to come.

"*El agua es sucio*," she said. The water is dirty. "*Oloroso*." It smelled. I knew those words now. I bent over the pail and agreed that it stank. Perhaps a rat had fallen between the cracks of the platform that held the pump. I said I would take a look and told her to forget the floors, and anything else that needed water. She left early.

When I had finished painting for the day, I found a rusty old crowbar from the shed, and after I'd scraped and swept the bird shit off, I started prying off the boards that covered the well. Some were rotted and almost flaked off; others appeared to have been recently replaced. I got them all off, pulled out the pipe, and got a flashlight. When I returned to the well, the parrot had returned, squawking from his perch on the pump handle, now leaning against the veranda.

The well wasn't deep, and my flashlight caught a shape much larger than a rat, clothed, bloated, and stinking. I called the real estate agent who then called the police. They were there within minutes, fishing the body out of the well. The parrot testified as they stowed the bagged body in the back of the vehicle and drove away.

2.

MARCO ALVAREZ SOTO had ridden all night; he and his horse dark silhouettes pounding along the shoreline, the low tide in their favour. At times, Isabella and the parrot loomed before him in the moonlight. He'd cried out, screamed at them, but the waves swallowed his mournful sounds, and he was alone with his misery, riding north. Tears diluted the blood that dripped down his face. At times he couldn't see, but the chestnut mare knew the route to his uncle's ranch. Exhausted, Marco was hanging onto the horse's mane when it stopped in front of the barn. He slid off, unsaddled the mare, and tethered her in the yard where flakes of hay lay scattered on the ground beside a full water trough. Marco stuck his head in the trough, washed his face, and dried it off with his red handkerchief, which came away darkened with blood. He felt his head; the gash had congealed and was starting to scab. He staggered to the barn and fell asleep on a pile of hay. He would explain in the morning.

The old man's gnarled hand was on his shoulder. When Marco opened his eyes and looked at his uncle hovering above him, bathed in light like an angel, he thought he was dreaming and that his uncle had passed on. He sat up, realizing it was mid-morning. Sunlight was pouring through the doorway backlighting his uncle. He clambered to his feet and hugged him; his uncle returned his embrace. Their frames trembled with emotion but neither said a word.

His uncle would wait to learn why his nephew wore a bloodied shirt and had a blood-encrusted scalp. Tío Vincente understood trouble. He'd served time for cattle rustling in his youth. He'd been mixed up with smugglers for several years, had made a lot of money, and had never been caught. But when his wife died several years ago of a heart attack, so had his criminal tendencies.

They walked back to the house and Tío Vincente poured them both coffee from a thermos. Vincente had never remarried, and by the neatness of the house, it appeared that either he had a housekeeper or he had become a domesticated widower. Marco sipped the steaming strong coffee, took a deep breath, and told his uncle as much as he could.

"I'm in a bit of hot water right now, Tío," he began. Another sip. "I have to leave Costa Rica and my farm, and disappear for a while. Can you help me?" His uncle's eyes were upon him, but he said nothing, just stroked his long white moustache and nodded for Marco to continue.

"I need you to call my parents, Tío. Tell them I had to go to Nicaragua. That they should sell the farm and keep the money. The deed is in my father's name anyway. Will you do that for me, Tío?"

Vincente agreed to call Marco's parents, and made the call in Marco's presence so he would know it had been done. Vincente was non-judgemental and didn't pry; he knew that Marco would tell him, or not, all in good time.

"Stay as long as you need, son," he told Marco. "Be good to have you around for a while." The old man was lonely and would enjoy his nephew's company. "Maybe you can help me prune some of the mango and avocado trees. All those branches I can't reach."

"Dad told me that you fell off the ladder last year and broke your arm. How's it feeling?"

"Oh, it's okay. Slow to mend at my age. I have to be careful."

"Sure thing, Tío. Anything you need. Be glad to help." Being active would distract him, reduce the time he spent thinking about Isabella. Like his father, his uncle was easy to be around. They were both comfortable in silence; they didn't need to talk all the time like other people who feared they'd disappear if they were silent.

Tío Vincente had become religious. He prayed before his meals and read the Bible in the evenings. Marco hadn't remembered this about him, but he hadn't spent much time with him since he was a kid. Marco bowed his head in respect at mealtimes, but his mind was not focused on God or the Blessed Virgin.

His uncle might be devout, but he still enjoyed a drink. One evening, they had two bottles of wine with dinner, and then Vincente pulled out a bottle of brandy from the sideboard. They leaned back in their chairs, cradling crystal snifters, reminiscing about their family. Vincente was talking about his wife.

"I'm certain I killed her, Marco," he said, swirling the cognac, looking into the glass for some kind of confirmation.

"How so, Tío?" Marco stuttered, gulping.

"From the work I was doing. When I was smuggling. Sonia thought it was dangerous work, and I guess it was, but I was sharp. It was early days, and the police weren't as wise as they are now. And they didn't have many boats on the water, so I felt fairly safe. I didn't realize how much she worried, Marco. I think the anxiety she had over what I was doing strained her heart and took her away from me." He sighed and raised the snifter to his lips. "I pray every day that she forgives me."

Marco looked away from his uncle to see Isabella standing in the doorway, the parrot perched on her shoulder. He blinked. She was gone. He shook his head, unable to discern what was real and what wasn't.

"What's the matter, son? You look like you've seen a ghost. I haven't upset you with this talk, have I?" Vincente leaned forward, put his hand on Marco's shoulder.

"No, no, Tío." Marco looked for the words. "You're right, though. I did just see a ghost. My wife." With that utterance,

Marco folded in a heap on the table, his shoulders trembling with sobs that wracked his body. Vincente stood and placed both of his hands on Marco's shoulders and mumbled some words that Marco didn't understand but that felt soothing, like the calming effects of a lullaby. When he'd stopped crying, he wiped his eyes and told his uncle what had happened, showed him the gash on his head, and explained why he was running. When he had finished, Vincente was stroking his long white moustache and looking off in the distance.

"It was a shock for me to hear that there are some women who abuse their men. We always think it's the other way around, but I've learned that both genders share this unharnessed anger, and though it is manifest for many of the same reasons, the abuse varies. A couple of my buddies used to come to work with black eyes and scratches on their arms. I didn't think much about it. I even joked with them about barroom brawls." Vincente leaned forward and gripped his crystal goblet with both hands. "It wasn't until one guy got his neck slashed with a machete, and when he claimed that his wife did it, the others admitted that their wives were rough with them, too." He tossed the last of his brandy back and reached for the bottle. "Other men are belittled, criticized, admonished for failing to provide for their families; that's abuse, too." As he poured, he continued. "There are all kinds of abuse, Marco, and some women wield their brand of it like swords: silent but deadly." He swirled his brandy, took a small sip. "Physical scars heal and all but disappear. But when the heart is scarred, the memory is always with you. Better to be beaten and suffer the blows than to be emotionally brutalized with hateful, degrading slashes to your character. That's hard to come back from."

3.

OH, YES, MARCO, I admit I had a temper. If I'd known, I might have been able to blame this particular outburst on hormones. Perhaps hormones are to blame for all of the rage that spewed from me over the years. But those emotions evaporated when I passed from this life. As I was dying, I saw a kaleidoscope of every tantrum I had thrown. I saw all of my outbursts and angry moments drift away with my last heartbeats. And after I sighed my last breath, my grandmother and grandfather, uncles, aunts, cousins—even friends who'd died and gone before me—appeared, welcoming me. Frozen in time, they looked the same as I had remembered them. We were all bathed in light. I left on the wind, the same breeze that blew through the mane of the horse you rode north.

I arrived at Tío Vincente's farm before you. The house was in darkness. I filled the water trough, broke a bale of hay apart, and set out flakes for your horse. I fluffed up the straw in the mow for you to sleep. I stayed with you that night, rubbing your back, wiping your brow, murmuring gently in your ear.

When you awoke in the morning and went to the house to have coffee with Tío Vincente, I drifted down the coast again. I returned to the house where we'd lived. I saw myself as you had left me, bloated in the well, barely recognizable. If there was an investigation, they would get no dental records because I have always had perfect teeth. And from being in the water so long, my fingerprints would probably be distorted, but since I don't have a criminal record, they would be useless to identify me anyway.

Our bedroom was a mess. Shards of broken glass lay scattered where they'd fallen, mineral stains marking the tiles where the water had pooled and dried on the floor. A strong gust of wind swept the glass into a corner. I found my cedula*—my photo identification card—and my passport in my purse on the bed. Another whirlwind lifted them into the air and carried them to a neighbour's yard where a small fire burned unattended. The wind calmed and dropped them into the flames where they bubbled, curled, and danced till they turned to ash and lifted into the sky once again. I checked the house thoroughly before I left. You had taken all of your identification, leaving nothing to identify us. Your parents hadn't lived there in more than twenty years, and the neighbouring properties had new owners, none of whom would remember the Alvarez hacienda, much less Marco or Isabella. Satisfied, I returned to Tío Vincente's farm.*

You'd finished dinner. I watched from the doorway of the dining room, listened to you talk, reminisce, getting drunker by the snifter. Your explanation was correct, Marco. Oh, how I wanted to apologize and free your conscience. I wanted to comfort you, to forgive you, but I knew your heart and mind were not of one accord. I nodded, agreeing with Tío Vincente, his observations of spousal abuse. We were both to blame, but the cause of my death was an accident.

I stayed with you, urging you to the truth.

I promise that I will set things right. You are protected, Marco; you will be happy again. And Tía Sonia will come to Vincente once again; she will embrace him and bathe him in forgiveness. Believe me.

4.

I WAS WRONG. I could kick myself for not having learned more Spanish. When Maria arrived a couple of days later, she brought a copy of *La Nación*, the major daily newspaper out of San José. She pointed to the article.

"*Una mujer, muy pequeña, delgada, como una niña.*"

"Small, like a child. *Como una niña*. Not a child." The discovery that it had been a woman plunged into the well, and not a child, did not diminish the brutality of the crime that had been committed. A crime against a woman, always horrific, sometimes had some crazed reasoning behind it. It could have been a crime of passion, hatred, vengeance, or jealousy. I liked to think that a child would not elicit such base emotions, but I was only somewhat relieved.

I poured Maria a mug of coffee and offered her a chair at the dining-room table where we spread the newspaper and I made notes in the margins, sorting out the story from Maria's translation. There would be an autopsy, but in addition to the woman's body being stuffed in the well, the journalist reported that a massive contusion on the back of the victim's head had been discovered, which made it debatable whether drowning was the cause of death. Her identity was still unknown. And because the body had been submerged in cold water, time of death was difficult to determine.

Detectives and their lackeys arrived to scour my property, the shoreline, the orchard, barn, shed, and of course, the house.

In the shed on a workbench under the broken pottery, they discovered a darning needle, a spool of thread, and a skein of lightweight Velcro-like ribbon. In a drawer I hadn't bothered to open, they found a number of empty tiny zip-lock bags like a jeweller might use to store repaired rings or chains, as well as a notebook with sketches of patterns for avian harnesses drawn in a child's notebook with a parrot on the cover. In the bedroom under a loose tile on the floor, they retrieved an empty cash box.

5.

IT WAS LATE AFTERNOON and Marco was just getting up in his darkened room in the Casa de Papel, located on a quiet street off the square in Liberia. He'd been awake most of the night, tormented by demons that had followed him from Tamarindo. They'd haunted him for weeks at his uncle's farm and continued to poke and prod him, screaming accusations, laughing maniacally. They had finally become quiet near dawn, a stalemate. They'd worn him down, and when he couldn't argue anymore, they'd let him sleep. Still tired, he showered, dressed, and walked a block to Pizza Pronto, a parlour the owner of the hotel had recommended.

Pizza Pronto baked in wood-fired stone ovens, adding a smoky flavour to the ingredients and an incomparable crunchiness to the crusts. Marco looked out at the ovens located in the corner of the main dining room. They reminded him of large round buttocks, mooning the customers. He ordered a glass of red wine and a medium pizza with chorizo, mushrooms, and olives. The owner was alone at the bar where he cashed out his patrons, and since it wasn't busy, he started chatting with Marco. Before his pizza arrived, they had covered the recent election outcome, soccer, and the weather. The delicious food, the distraction of his surroundings, and the mindless conversation had soothed him somewhat, had slowed the Formula One car that had been racing in his mind since last night. The press coverage he'd read the previous morning at breakfast, seated among strangers in the dining room, had been unnerving. He'd almost choked on his orange juice. That information had been swirling in his head since then and hadn't let up. The wine was helping to soften the edges of his jagged memories.

He'd arrived at Pizza Pronto early; at first, the only customer. Now the place was filling with diners, and conversation and music fused into a cacophonous buzz like a new species of cicada. He finished the last mouthful of wine, paid the bill, and left. But he still hadn't achieved the level of numbness he sought.

At Hotel Liberia, he ordered a cognac and sat in the garden where he could legally smoke a cigarette in peace. It was a space the owner provided that was the legally required distance from the building, even though it was inside his establishment.

Later, when his head hit the pillow, he passed out, snoring like a vociferous pig. In the middle of the night, he awoke dehydrated and knocked over the lamp and his cellphone before he found his bottle of water on the night table. When he slept again, the lime green parrot visited him, landing on his shoulder.

"*Ya vengo, Don Marco. Todo bien. Fue un éxito. Mucho dinero. Ja, ja, ja.*" The bird dropped from Marco's shoulder onto his lap, marked time like a marching soldier, and dutifully lifted its wings ever so slightly. Marco released Don Verde from the miniature Velcro harness that fit snugly under his wings, and over his back and breast. He unfastened the nylon mesh pouch from the harness and unfolded an international money order for twenty thousand dollars and a bogus "paid in full" invoice for architectural design. The bird flew out of his dream and Marco slept deeply.

The next morning, at breakfast, when the sun rose over the walls of the hacienda, a large photograph of a field that hung on a west wall came to life as the sun bathed it in light. Marco had worked out a reasonable deal with the owner of the Casa de Papel and planned to stay for a month. He loved the Old World ambience of the hacienda, home to the owner's family for three generations. The outside walls were papered with newspaper clippings and photographs of bygone days. Enlarged photographs hung from the walls of the reception area and the lounge. By the pool and dining area, there were more photographs of farm implements, their antique subjects displayed around the patio.

Over the course of the next few days, Marco had finally started to relax. He floated in the pool for hours each afternoon, exercised on the lawn, and gazed at cloud formations as they passed over him while he lounged poolside. He tried not to think, but to empty his mind and drift like the clouds. In the evenings, he went to Hotel Liberia, which had a good dining room and a pleasant smoking garden.

6.

I STARTED TO BUY *La Nación* regularly, to see if I could learn more Spanish and to keep an eye on the reportage of the murder, if that was what it had been. I listened intently to the parrot that told me his name was Don Verde. The bird seemed to speak in three separate, distinct voices: one, almost androgynous, that said "*no me pegues,*" which meant "don't hit me." Another sounded like a woman whimpering. The third was the distinct voice of a man yelling "*cállete,*" which meant "shut up." Then the voice gave instructions, cautions, and blessings for travel. And I didn't need to look up what "*mucho dinero*" meant.

The detectives hadn't paid much attention to the parrot, but after they'd bagged all they could find that was of interest, they came out to see what I was doing and that's when they heard Don Verde speak. I offered my opinion about his voices, and they sat down. I brought out mugs and poured them coffee from my thermos. They sipped and waited, obviously enjoying the offshore breeze and the rhythmic crashing waves on the shore.

They remained quiet around the table, but just as they were making moves to leave, Don Verde started reciting his litany again. Notebooks came out. A cellphone with a tape recorder was turned on, and they stayed for at least an hour, encouraging the bird to tell them more, and to repeat phrases, as if Don Verde could explain what he was saying. The chief detective had suggested taking the parrot as a witness, but as soon as he had uttered the words, Don Verde streaked into the trees and remained silent, not returning until long after they'd left.

7.

THE ARTICLE SAID that detectives had found blood on the corner of the desk. Its shape matched the contusion on the back of the body's head. They said the woman had probably fallen against it. The autopsy would determine the cause of death.

Marco knew that Isabella had died in his arms. Still, he'd given her an unorthodox burial. He was guilty of lunging at her, causing her to fall. But in the three years that they'd been together, he'd had his share of her physical abuse. After he read through the article a second time, he flipped mindlessly through the rest of the newspaper, methodically turning pages while reliving their last argument. They'd been eating breakfast. Don Verde had been screaming and Isabella was whining about something. She had wanted to buy a car, Marco remembered. She complained that she hated taking buses. *Dios mio*. She didn't even know how to drive. The parrot had continued to yap, and he'd wanted it to shut up. Marco yelled at him, chased him, and the bird flew onto the veranda but kept screaming. Isabella stomped out of the room. For a little woman she was feisty. He remembered her bare feet pounding the floor as she went to the bedroom, continuing to scream at him. He followed her, and she ripped flowers out of a cut glass vase and had thrown the vase at his head. He fell on the bed, stunned and bleeding. When he stood up, she was still yelling. He staggered over to her, but before he got near enough to touch her, she slipped on the wet tiles and fell.

He'd been angry for a number of reasons, but all of those reasons had fused together, building and building until he exploded. They'd wanted to have a family. That was also part of his frustration. Maybe he had been shooting blanks all this time, or maybe her eggs were infertile. Whatever the reason, try as they might—marking the calendar for her ovulations, trying to get home when she called—she still couldn't get pregnant.

"Don't hit me. Please don't hit me," the parrot often yelled in a voice that was neither Isabella's nor Marco's, but a combination of their intonations. There were times when Marco had pleaded for Isabella not to hit him. And she'd pummelled him. He admitted to slapping her but never with a closed fist. They'd had their moments. He remembered the sound of her head hitting the corner of the desk that night, a deadening thud. Her beautiful long hair had absorbed most of the blood. But she hadn't woken up. He splashed cold water on her face, patted her cheeks and talked to her, urging her back. He felt her neck for a pulse, but she was gone. He sat beside her for a long time, stroking her hair and crying, while drops of his blood fell on her blouse. Then fear joined him on the floor. He wrestled with the ugly creature until it finally left him and he knew what had to be done.

One morning, a few days into his stay in Liberia, Marco decided to eat breakfast at Hotel Liberia, where he could sit alone and read *La Nación*, instead of being one among a table of strange lodgers at Casa de Papel. He was alone in the dining room when he opened the paper to a new article. The coroner had determined more than the cause of Isabella's death, which was confirmed to be a contusion and cracked skull from falling. The second discovery he'd made was that she had been pregnant—two months—at the time of her death. As Marco read the words, his body quaked like it would erupt, his shoulders trembled, and then he burst into tears.

He quickly ran to the bathroom, his hands over his mouth to stifle the explosive sobbing. His knees bent like willows in a windstorm. He grabbed the wall for support. All the voices in his head were screaming to such a high pitch that he covered his ears, but that didn't silence them.

When he finally stopped crying, he was exhausted. He splashed some water on his face and mopped it with a paper towel. He went back to his table, carried his coffee to the garden, and lit a cigarette. Pregnant. He was going to be a father. Past tense. Was. No more. When he'd finished his coffee and paid the bill, he walked to the square and looked up the dozen or so whitewashed steps to the Immaculata Concepción church, a stark white structure gleaming like a beacon. The last time Marco had entered a church was last December, to say goodbye to his grandfather; the time before that, his wedding three years ago. He walked across the square and climbed the steps. Unlike other somber, dark churches he'd been in, this one was bright and airy, filled with light. He used the main entrance but saw there were open doors on each side of the nave. Sunlight streamed through the stained glass windows, and additional lighting illuminated the enormous gold cross above the altar, echoed by a smaller version below the chancel. He walked up the centre aisle; at the altar he genuflected, crossed himself, and then went to the small chapel at the north of the altar. He folded two twenty-dollar bills into the donations box and struck a long match.

"I don't have much experience praying, Lord," Marco began. "I haven't been to confession since I was a teenager, and I have done some terrible things for which I am truly sorry. I fought with my wife, and she fell and died. I was afraid, God, so I hid her and ran. That is unforgivable." He held the match over one of the candles.

"Isabella, my beautiful wife, I pray that you find peace and comfort in Heaven. I pray that you will forgive me one day." He held the match over the wick of the second votive. "To our unborn child: please know that you were created out of love and our loving ways. I pray that your spirit will be protected until it is time for you to come again." He blew out the match and bowed his head for a few seconds before he turned to leave. Halfway down the centre aisle, he stopped and returned to the chapel. He put another twenty-dollar bill in the box and lit another match.

"One more thing, dear God: I ask you to save my miserable soul." He lit the candle, crossed himself, then turned and left the church. He stood on the top step and breathed deeply. When he exhaled, he felt lighter. His shoulders dropped from their hunching position close to his ears, and when he moved his neck, it cracked for the first time in longer than he could remember.

That night he slept soundly. When he awoke, he distinctly remembered two dreams: in one, Isabella was caressing his face. She was smiling and radiant. The second was a little spirit that floated in the sky above the clouds, drifting, seemingly contented. He was surprised to feel so fresh and rested. Before anyone else in the hotel had roused, he dipped into the pool and soundlessly stretched and manoeuvred his muscles until the first of the guests arrived for breakfast. He had started a new regime: after breakfast and before reading the newspaper, he walked up to the square and visited the church, to light three candles. It couldn't hurt, he thought.

8.

I WATCHED YOU light the candles, Marco. I listened to your thoughts when you prayed for me and asked my forgiveness. I wanted to breathe on the candle—not to blow it out, but to give you a sign that I was with you. But I remained still, bathed in your love, saddened by your remorse.

"Oh, yes, Marco. I forgive you." My lips moved though you couldn't hear me. "And I will show you how much I love you. You will see."

I lingered in the chancel as you left. The setting brought back memories of my childhood when I went to convent school in Cartago. When you lit the candles, I remembered when I was a little girl, getting up at four o'clock in the morning, shivering while I wrapped paper around my candle so the wax wouldn't drip on my fingers when we walked in procession down the dark cobblestone street to the church for mass. Life was strict and rigid then. It was what made me strong, determined, and disciplined in my brief adult life on earth.

9.

AFTER THE AUTOPSY and an investigation that seemed to have led nowhere, I received the okay to have the well pumped, disinfected, and put back in working order. If only for emergencies, it was good to know there was a backup supply should something happen with the municipal waterline again. Meanwhile, life continued.

I resumed painting. I pruned trees and cultivated a garden of tomatoes, onions, basil, and cilantro, all of which became staples in my kitchen. Don Verde was still a regular on the pump handle, but he never came inside. I had carried his cage out onto the veranda and would put a flowering plant in it if he didn't want to use it anymore. Why would he, if he was free to roam and roost wherever he wanted? I imagined that the previous owners had kept his wings clipped but then remembered the harness and his former career. How far would he have flown? How did he know the route? I knew that parrots were smart, could differentiate colours, textures, and numbers, but I'd never heard of parrots being used as mules.

10.

"WHAT'S KEEPING YOU?" It was Antonio Vargas, calling from Granada, Nicaragua. Antonio was not one for pleasantries. He got right to the point. That was his style.

"What do you mean? I'm taking some time off. I didn't think anything was happening. What's the rush?"

"Get yourself to the border, and I'll tell you then."

"There's no bus until tomorrow morning. It gets to the border around eleven."

"See you then."

Marco caught the Ticabus on the highway outside Hotel El Bromadero at 9:40 the next morning. As always, the bus was full with a mix of Nicas going home, Ticos going shopping, and expats and tourists doing their visa runs before their ninety-day visas expired in Costa Rica. They'd cross the border into Nicaragua and stay somewhere for a few days, and after having their passports stamped, they were welcome to return to Costa Rica for another ninety days. Marco was a Tico and had both his *cedula,* which proved his Costa Rican citizenship, and his passport. He could have taken the bus directly to Granada, saving Antonio some travel time, but he must have had a reason for meeting him, and nothing beat the comfort of Antonio's Mercedes-Benz 450SL. The car was shining like a silver vessel in the dusty gravel parking lot at Peñas Blancas, at the border between Costa Rica and Nicaragua, when his bus pulled into Immigration.

"Good to see you, Marco. You're looking good." They shook hands and hugged, slapped each other on the back. Antonio slid back into the car and opened the sunroof.

"I went to see my uncle, helped him a little, and then kicked back for a few weeks at a hotel in Liberia. Got some rest." Antonio knew that Marco had left Tamarindo in a hurry, but he didn't know the details.

Antonio and Marco's smuggling projects were unique. Each one was different so that no patterns could be followed if the police were watching. They never used the same route or method of transport, but air and water were favoured over land. There was, however, one anomaly: Marco had a talented green parrot that he had used intermittently to mule small packets of cocaine to boys on freighters anchored in the waters near Marco's house. He'd done this successfully on a regular basis, over a few months.

Marco had been inspired by stories about his grandfather training and using carrier pigeons to send communications during the five-year war against the U.S. Marines in Nicaragua. Antonio remembered visiting Marco and watching him train the bird. He'd anchored a dinghy a few feet out in the water off his place at Tamarindo, and set slices of bright orange mango on the sides of the craft. In another dinghy, he rowed out to it, encouraging Don Verde to fly with him, over to his treat. It was amazing—just like a homing pigeon. Maybe there had been complications. He'd learn of them if Marco felt the need to tell him.

"Ready to go again?" Antonio grinned, nudging him in the ribs as he moved his arm to shift into reverse.

"That depends." Silence. But when Marco looked over at Antonio, he saw that he was smiling. An hour up the Pan-American Highway they exited for San Juan del Sur on the Pacific coast. They parked outside a marina, ordered two espressos at the bar, and carried them out to the patio where there were a couple of tables with umbrellas unfurled. The wind off the ocean splashed against the docks, nudging the boats in a rhythmic movement, background for a chorus of screaming gulls. Antonio shook a packet of sugar into his cup, stirred it with a little wooden stick. Blew on it before daring a sip. He nodded at the boats in the marina.

"See that forty-foot sloop down there: *Dulce Sueños*? Next to the catamaran?"

"What about it?"

"It has a hollowed-out compartment in the hull."

"That so?"

"It's leaving in a couple of weeks for Puerto Arista in Chiapas, Mexico, on a leisurely family sail to visit some friends."

"And do we have some interest in this leisurely cruise?" Marco leaned back in his chair, curious, but aloof. He finished the dregs of his espresso and crumpled the flimsy paper cup in his fist.

"Only a little way up the coast. The captain is your cousin, and you'll be hitching a ride. At a harbour slip in Puerto Sandino, where they will drop you off, you'll meet with the captain of another vessel. He'll invite you aboard for a drink. You'll exchange merchandise for money and Hector Cortez and his seaplane will meet you and take you back to the docks in Granada. Good plan, no?"

"Better than that yappy bird."

"Don Verde made us a lot of money, Marco. Admit it."

"Okay. He did. But he *cost* me a lot more than money can buy." Marco didn't elaborate, and Antonio didn't push it. Bottom line was that the bird had muled for them, and they'd raked in close to a hundred thousand dollars on those wings.

When Antonio had finished his coffee, they climbed back into the Mercedes and drove further north, but east this time, to San Jorge, in the municipality of Rivas. Antonio pulled into the parking lot of the Hotel Hamacas, got out and opened the trunk. He pulled out a duffle bag and looked at Marco. "Come on. Grab your bag. We've got reservations."

Marco reluctantly climbed out and reached for his bag.

Antonio had reserved a suite near the pool. After raiding the bar fridge, they walked out to the terrace and watched a tour boat filled with tourists motor by on Lake Nicaragua. The sun illuminated the canvas roof like highly polished lapis lazuli.

"I have another job for you before the *Dulce Sueños.* A launch like the one down there is headed for Isla Ometepe tomorrow, and you will be one of the passengers. It'll take you an hour or so to get over there. You'll be carrying a backpack that I've got in my duffel bag. You'll stop for lunch on the island at a particular restaurant that the crew has chosen ahead of time. You'll be wearing a New York Yankees baseball cap—it's also in my bag—and the owner of the restaurant who stands at the entrance to greet his customers will comment on your good choice of team, that his grandson plays for them. He slaps you on the back. Don't worry if there's anyone else wearing a Yankees cap. The owner will recognize your backpack because he has one that's identical. Your group will have a reserved number of tables, but first, you decide to use the toilet. So you don't go to the table and leave your bag. Remember that. The owner will leave his greeting post when you're all inside and go back to the kitchen where he has hidden his bag under a pile of dirty linens. He'll carry it in the direction of the laundry room, but will duck into the washroom and meet you there. You will exchange bags. Check in the bag that the money is there—count it. Should be fifty thousand U.S. dollars. Then you can go back to the dining room and enjoy your beer and fried fish. Good, no?"

"You've even ordered for me?"

"No, no. Order what you want. But you get the picture, right?"

11.

ANTONIO VARGAS WAS an idea man, always plotting, scheming, and devising ways to make money. Since childhood, when he sold pencils on the street, he'd worked hard, refining his techniques. His family had been dirt poor then. So, he'd always been hungry, which had made him determined to make enough money to eat, to take some córdobas to his mother at the end of the day so she could buy tortillas and beans. His desperation had made him creative. He was ten years old when he'd first started selling pencils. The revolution to put an end to the Somoza regime had been waging for four years, many of which he had spent with his grandmother in Masaya. But he began to long for Granada and Lake Nicaragua, and had risked going home to stay with his parents.

Antonio Vargas was the great-nephew of General Augusto Sandino. His grandmother was proud of her brother and regaled Antonio and anyone who would listen, with stories about his endeavours. He was a national hero, who, in the late 1920s, had fought a five-year war against the U.S. military occupation of Nicaragua from the mountains of Segovia in the north of the country. One historian had described his army as "small and crazy"—no more than a band of impassioned farmers. But ferocious fighters they'd been for they'd ultimately ousted the Americans. Antonio's great-uncle met with President Juan Bautista Sacasa and pledged his support for the new government on the condition that the National Guard, headed by General

Anastasio Somoza would be dismantled and Sandino's men granted amnesty. But he was tricked. A month later, General Sandino was assassinated, under orders given by Somoza. Sandino had sparked the torch, though, and his name was honoured when the Sandinista National Liberation Front formed in 1961 to fight against the Somoza dictatorship. Anastasio Somoza Garcia was assassinated in 1956, but his two sons carried on, first Luis, for ten years, and then Anastasio Somoza Debayle until 1979, when Antonio was a child.

When he first started selling pencils, he had meandered along streets and often hadn't met anyone. Then he had gone to the market where the avenue teemed with bustling, jostling humanity. He walked down one side of the street bumping into people who were so much taller than he was. He listened to the clever chants the hawkers sang and made one up for himself.

"*Escribe bonitas palabras con estos lapiceros, muy barato. Compra unos para su esposo, sus niños, toda la familia, por un precio muy barato.*" Write nice words with these pencils very cheap. Buy some for your husband, your children, the whole family, for a very cheap price. Antonio's voice rang sweet and clear. Women smiled at him and opened their purses.

Then he'd gotten the idea that he should go to venues that specialized in words and numbers, and where everyone required pencils. So instead of spending precious time walking up and down the congested market, hoping that someone might need a pencil or buy one from him out of pity, he decided to go to nearby schools early in the morning where he'd be sure to sell more of his inventory than leaving it to chance. From schools he progressed to banks. He stood outside one each day, and just before they opened, several of the employees purchased his wares on their way in to work.

His deep brown eyes, warm smile, and friendly demeanour had served him well over the years. He'd always kept his curly black hair cut close to his head and never swayed to the fad of growing dreadlocks, which his curly hair would do, nor to growing it long, like a Jimi Hendrix afro. Though his clothes had often been patched or threadbare hand-me-downs from his older brother, they were spotless. Every night he stripped, wrapped a towel around his waist, and washed his one suit of clothes. And whenever he had shoes that would fit him, he kept them polished so bright he could see his reflection in them. His mother had brought him up well. He knew how to make *tamales* and *sopas* and how to cook a chicken—when they had money to buy one.

One morning after the banks had opened, when he had taken a break and was counting his money on a bench in Parque Central, his life changed. He was fourteen years old.

A rich architect from León had been watching him from a bench a few feet away. He had been reading a newspaper, but when Antonio sat down, he looked up, and curious, continued watching as the boy counted his money. Antonio put the money in his back pocket, and then picked up a greasy brown paper wrapper from the ground beside the bench, one that had held tortillas or hot churros, long gone. He smoothed it out and took one of his sharpened pencils from his pack and started sketching. Engrossed in his design, Antonio didn't notice the man standing behind him, looking down at the sketch.

"That's very good," the man said. It was the façade of the Hotel Alhambra across the street. Antonio looked up at the handsome man in his bright white cotton pants, his Panama hat.

"Thank you, sir. Would you like to buy a pencil?" Antonio slid the case of pencils at the man who smiled. He sat down beside Antonio. He smelled good.

"Do you go to school?" the man asked. Antonio looked down at his hands and shook his head.

"No. My family can't afford the uniforms, books, or supplies. My brother went for a while. Now he works with my uncle on his farm in Segovia." Antonio looked down the busy Calle La Calzada to the lake.

"I haven't had breakfast yet," the man said. "Would you

like to join me?" Antonio had never eaten in a restaurant. He nodded, and they both stood and walked down Calle La Calzada to a restaurant that was serving outside. Antonio watched every move the man made. He ordered coffee for them both, and when it arrived, Antonio watched the man rip open a paper envelope and pour the sugar into his coffee. Antonio did the same. That morning, he learned more etiquette than he'd ever seen practised in his life. The man—his name was Ricardo Gómez—told him that he was an architect and had his own business in his home in León. Antonio had heard of the city but had never been there.

"I could use a talented draftsman like you—that's what you're called when you sketch buildings. A draftsman. What do you think? Would you like to be my apprentice?" Antonio nodded enthusiastically.

Señor Gómez drove Antonio home to discuss his proposition with Antonio's parents. Antonio smiled and waved at his friends when they drove over the dusty streets of the *barrio* in the low-slung Mercedes. He introduced Señor Gómez to his mother and father, and the man told them what he proposed. They were so happy they cried. Antonio knew they were thinking about one less mouth to feed, and the possibility that he'd send money home—both true. He was proud to think that he could do something so important for them. That day, Antonio ended his career selling pencils and drove off with the rich handsome man to live in León in a beautiful house where he would earn money, have all the food he wanted, and sleep in a bed, not a mattress on a dirt floor.

The house was what Señor Gómez called a colonial design, built by one of the rich Spaniards who'd come to their new colony. On the landing of the wide Honduran mahogany staircase, the sun shone through panels of stained glass; the scene was an apple orchard in bloom with contented sheep grazing beneath the trees. Antonio and Señor Gómez dined in a room in the centre of the house that was filled with trees, flowering hibiscus, and caged songbirds. At one end of the long wooden table, Antonio sat in a comfortable chair that had a padded seat and arms. Señor Gómez sat at the other end. That night he'd eaten until his stomach ached.

"Will you miss your friends, Antonio?" Señor Gómez asked him.

"No not really. I didn't have much time to play."

"Do you have a girlfriend?" Señor Gómez asked. His smile reminded Antonio of a fox. He'd shoved back his chair and was walking over to Antonio. Antonio felt his face heating up.

"No, señor. No time for that either." His face was hot, but he didn't know why. He was telling the truth. He didn't have a girlfriend.

"Oh, I hope you're able to make time now," Señor Gómez said.

"What about you, señor? Are you married? Do you have a family?" He looked up at the man who towered over him.

"Ah, no. I'm happy as a bachelor. Women really don't interest me." His hands rubbed Antonio's shoulders. It felt good.

"Let me show you to your room," he said, pulling out Antonio's chair for him.

They walked together up the wide staircase. The sheep were no longer visible, dormant in the darkness. Señor Gómez draped his arm over Antonio's shoulder, his slender fingers caressing Antonio's collarbone. "Your room is right here, Antonio. Mine is just down the hall. Don't hesitate to call if you need anything," he said, and opened the door. Antonio slid out from under the oppressive arm and walked quickly to the bathroom where he shut the door, considered locking it, and then opened it again, though he stood behind it.

"Thank you, Señor Gómez. You're very kind. Good night, sir."

"Good night, Antonio. Sleep well."

And he did.

Antonio had had his own drafting table with a globe of light suspended above it and a high swivel chair. His feet barely touched the floor. His first exercise had been to sketch a building from a photograph Señor Gómez had given him. As he drew, he could hear Señor Gómez in his office talking on the telephone about a project. When he hung up, he came out to see Antonio. He stood behind him with his hands on Antonio's shoulders again, thankfully interrupted when the phone rang.

Señor Gómez had clients all over the country and often Antonio was left alone in the house for days, with only the housekeeper for company. He didn't mind. He was comfortable and didn't have to worry about money. And the absence of worry allowed him to be even more creative—without being desperate. On his drafting table, Señor Gómez had left a telephone number where he could be reached if there was an emergency. He'd written the number on one of his ruined invoices, a blotch of ink smeared over the figures. Antonio looked at the layout of the invoice, and with a fresh piece of paper, he created his own invoice: Vargas Architectural Consulting, complete with a logo of which the V, A, and C towered above the other letters. He made up an address in Granada, added a telephone number, and when he was finished, filed his creation with the money he was saving.

Señor Gómez taught him how to open a bottle of wine. On his fifteenth birthday, he learned how to uncork a bottle of champagne without shooting the cork into the air and losing the precious contents. He learned how to make a tossed salad, to carve a roast of beef, and at Christmas, a turkey. He put the knowledge to use when he stayed alone and sometimes prepared a meal for the housekeeper. He invited her to join him in the dining room, which she reluctantly agreed to, but she was too timid to sit in Señor Gómez' chair. Instead, she sat at a corner of the table, close to Antonio.

One evening, Antonio had gone to bed and was asleep when Señor Gómez returned. Drunk. He listened as Señor Gómez fumbled with Antonio's door and the next thing he knew he was sprawled beside him, trying to get his hand under the covers that Antonio held tight to his body. Señor Gómez soon passed out, snoring, on the bed beside him. Antonio had waited until he felt sure that Señor Gómez wouldn't wake up, and then, he snaked out from under the bedcovers. He dressed quickly, pulled the money and notes from his bureau, and carried his shoes downstairs. He put them on and fled with nothing but the clothes on his back and the money he had saved. He had more than enough to buy food, a bus ticket back to Granada, with some left over to get him through a few days—even if he had to stay in a hostel.

Antonio remembered when he had first met Señor Gómez that he'd thought it was strange that such a handsome man would not be married. He cursed himself, feeling foolish, when he finally realized Señor Gómez was a homosexual, and was probably looking for something more than Antonio could give him. He had taken the next bus back to Granada that night and vowed never to put himself in a vulnerable position again. He had further promised himself that he would work for no one, that he would be his own boss.

Antonio Vargas had lived up to that twenty-five-year-old promise. When he returned to Granada, he'd gone to stay with an older friend who lived alone, instead of going home. His parents would have wanted an explanation. They'd be disappointed in the return of their son. If he told them the truth, would they have believed him? He doubted it. In their eyes, rich people could do no wrong.

He'd started dealing marijuana and made enough to pay for a room and food. Then he met Marco Alvarez Soto and his life changed again. They were both into dealing and met for the first time in a café near where they both made their purchases. Ten years ago, they each had only just made ends meet, but after pooling their wits, stealth, and energies, they'd more than quadrupled their profits. Antonio had registered Vargas Architectural Consulting and used the invoices to document the large sums of money they received from selling drugs. Faithfully, he reported the income from his consulting firm and paid taxes: a small price to pay.

12.

THE TOUR BOATS left from a wharf near the ferry terminal, and the schedules for both were regular; his was at ten o'clock. Marco would have preferred the stability of the larger craft but that would have wrecked the scenario Antonio had masterminded with the restaurant owner. The winds whipped the canvas roof of the *Lancha* and sprayed mist on the passengers sitting closest to the bow. As they left the dock, whitecaps licked the lake; craft that were tied or moored in the harbour bobbled and nudged each other, safe only from the bumpers and tires that hung along their gunnels. Luckily, Marco had a strong stomach and could withstand the rough waters as well as the occasional retching of passengers who could not.

Two men sat together near the driver of the launch. They didn't look like tourists even though they were dressed in tropical shirts and Panama hats. Unlike the other passengers, who gawked at the view through their binoculars and cameras, the two men looked straight ahead or leaned their heads close, talking to each other, their mirrored Foster Grants giving nothing away. Marco sensed they were undercover cops. Tonio hadn't bargained for this little glitch in the scenario, he thought. He set his backpack between his feet and turned to the fair-haired young couple who sat beside him on the bench.

"Have you been to Ometepe Island before?" he asked them in English.

"Oh, you speak English!" the young man said, and he and his girlfriend smiled and turned in their seats so they could both see him.

"We're from California," the girl added. "This is my husband, Corky, and I'm Amanda." Then Corky put his arm around Amanda, and she grinned. "We just got married. We're on our honeymoon. It's our first time here."

And thus, a conversation began that diverted Marco's attention from the two suspicious-looking men and helped pass the time until they docked at the port in Moyogalpa. They were in the centre of the craft, and when it tied up at the dock, they were out before the balance of passengers. They walked up Calle Santa Ana to a cross street and saw the sign for Los Ranchitos, the restaurant where their guide had made reservations. They continued to talk, Marco explaining as best he could what he'd learned about the island. By the time the rest of the passengers disembarked, including the two men in the Foster Grants, Marco and the newlyweds were a block ahead of them. As they neared Los Ranchitos, Marco adjusted his New York Yankees baseball cap to better shade his eyes. As Antonio had predicted, the owner stood at the entrance to the restaurant, the palm frond roof towering over the chubby little Nicaraguan. He smiled as the three of them approached.

"Good choice of team, my young man." He slapped Marco on the back. "My grandson plays for the Yankees." He nodded and smiled at the owner. Before he entered the restaurant with his new friends, Marco cast a furtive look back down the street. The other passengers were still a block away. The owner saw the direction Marco was looking in and returned his nod.

The three of them were directed to one of two reserved tables. Marco thanked the waiter and told Amanda and Corky that he needed to use the facilities, to order him a Toña, and that he'd join them in a moment. Before he opened the door to the men's room, he glanced back. The owner had left the entrance. Marco entered a cubicle but left the door open a crack to be able to see who entered. Isabella appeared at the doorway, then disappeared. A moment later, the owner opened the door of the washroom. Marco joined him in the middle of the room where they traded backpacks. Marco counted the money and was satisfied. They shook hands. The old man left first with the backpack hidden in the towels. Marco joined the newlyweds at their table. He looked around for the men in the Foster Grants but didn't see them.

"Didn't everyone come to this restaurant?" Marco asked Amanda and Corky.

"The owner just came by and told us that one of the guys—one of the two guys who sat near us on the boat—tripped in a pothole and broke his ankle. His friend went with him in a taxi to the medical clinic. They'll take another launch back to San Jorge."

13.

I REALIZED THAT THIS would be the second Christmas that I would spend alone. Last year, the divorce had been so fresh and I felt so raw, tender, and humiliated, that I'd avoided all social interaction during the season, save talking with Nathan my grocer, who also baked bread, had a great selection of fruits and vegetables, cut his own roasts, and stocked my favourite wines. I'd stayed clear of Fifth Avenue, the joyful carols, and the glittering window displays. I hadn't ventured any further than my grocer and the video stores—both of which delivered, though I never reached that level of reclusiveness. I think my friends understood that I needed space, and they gave it to me. No big dinner parties; just an occasional drop-in from a buddy who always knew when to leave. The season passed, and I made it over that social hurdle.

This year wouldn't be difficult at all. The commercial aspect of Christmas probably flourished in the urban centres of Liberia and San Jose, but I was in a virtually rural part of the country. Only the hotels along the beach might have an artificial tree in the lobby, or tinsel garlands strung along the banisters, or carols playing over the sound system—recognizable carols, but in Spanish and with a Latin rhythm. I would treat the day like any other and follow my usual routine. The only aspect of the season I observed was giving Maria, as well as the mail and garbage men, their customary Christmas envelopes, a small stipend to go along with the gratitude I had for the good work they'd done over the year, even though I hadn't been here for much of it. Still, it was a good investment in the future.

I'd only been living in Costa Rica for two months now, but I'd been painting virtually every day except for the time around the investigation. I had painted eight new canvases and after I photographed them, I sent them to a gallery in New York. The owner of the gallery had been to my last exhibition and was impressed with my work. But more than a year had passed since then; perhaps there was a new popular flavour in the New York art world. Regardless, I wouldn't stop painting, and, as an old friend once told me, my work would find its audience.

Don Verde figured prominently in several of my paintings. The harness fascinated me, but the investigation was ongoing, and I had been advised not to reveal anything about it. Maybe later. For now, the lime green parrot flitted through the foliage in my work, often so camouflaged by the greens in the vines and the leaves of the trees that locating him was like the game, *Where's Waldo?* The feathered critic Don Verde often sat nearby, chuckling, mumbling, and at times sounding surprisingly like me. He must listen to me talking on the phone and to Maria. He'd perfected Maria's "*Dios mio,*" and hummed like she did when she cleaned. With those new additions to his vocabulary, we heard fewer of the fearful expressions from his previous life.

14.

IT WAS MID-MORNING. Not a cloud in the sky; the sun played on the rippling water where gulls attempted to skim minnows feeding on the surface. A police cruiser on patrol slowly entered the marina gates at Puerto Sandino. The car's tires crunched over oyster shells that gravelled the driveway. They slowed at the first speed bump—both the driver and his partner lifting large sweating containers up from their laps as they did so. They lowered them and resumed sipping as the car rolled over the bump.

"Seems everyone has a different name for these things," the driver said, referring to the speed bumps. He sucked on his *batido*, with a loud slurping noise.. "In Mexico, they call speed bumps *topes*. Ticos call them *vibradores*, especially the ones that make a noise when you drive over them. Their other name for them is *redución de velocidad*." He inhaled the last of his milkshake and threw the container out the window. "And here, we tell it like it is, eh Juan Carlos? *Oficial dormido*." Sleeping officer. They both laughed.

They continued over the last speed bump and slowly approached the docks on a circular drive that extended past several aquatic berths where boats were tied like horses in their stalls. Seahorses, the driver thought, chuckling to himself. His partner lit a cigarette and exhaled through his open window. The officer slid his hands up and down the wheel as he gazed dreamily at the woman leaning over to wipe the far edge of a table on the patio at the marina restaurant. He groaned, groped his groin, silently urging the woman to lean further. His partner was oblivious, trying to blow smoke rings and failing badly. A man disembarked from a yacht with a backpack slung over his shoulder. He waved at the people who remained on board. It was probably the movement of their waving arms that caught the attention of the police officers. A plane was drifting in on the waves at the end of the docks. Another man on a yacht fifty metres away waved at the man with the backpack who appeared to hasten his step. The officer looked at his partner.

"Suspicious?"

"Yes, sir. Could be."

"Let's take a look." As they moved along the drive, a flock of seagulls swooped over the cruiser. They hovered, seemingly caught on the breeze above the car. They squawked, cawed, screamed at the officers as they hung on the breeze, effortlessly evacuating their bowels on the windshield, which was instantly iced with a snowy layer of *guano* resembling sour cream, ashes, and mustard. The slow-moving cruiser ground its tires into the oyster shells and stopped.

"See if you can get a pail," the driver told his partner. He flicked on the windshield wipers and washer fluid sprayed beyond the windshield and onto the partner's sleeve before he got away from the car. On the windshield, the excrement smeared and diluted with each release of fluid, reducing it to thinner and thinner layers like skimmed milk. The partner wiped at his uniform as he walked down to the dock with a pail he'd picked up on the path. He kneeled down on the dock and dipped the pail in the ocean. He eased the full pail up and out of the water, still partially stooped. Before he righted himself, a seagull swooped down, possibly curious about the embroidered epaulet on the man's shoulder and pecked at it. The driver stood outside the idling cruiser. He adjusted his sunglasses, looking down at the dock just as his partner capsized with the full pail in his hand. When he resurfaced, coughing and sputtering, his partner gave him a hand to climb out. He had one foot on the dock and was pulling himself up when another gull dive-bombed them both. The full pail of water sat on the planked dock, while the men splashed into the water. They used the ladder of a nearby boat to climb out, their uniforms dripping, their boots filled with water. The plane at the end of the wharf was taxiing out into the channel. Seated beside the pilot was the backpack guy. He waved as they became airborne. Hector Cortez, the pilot Antonio had hired, couldn't be heard above the roar of the plane's engine. Instead, he smiled and pointed to a cooler full of beer on the floor, Marco's refreshments for the flight back to Granada.

15.

MY PHONE RANG only days after I'd emailed the images of my paintings to the gallery in New York. "Simon Patrick," I answered.

"You certainly know how to warm a New Yorker's heart in the midst of a bitterly cold dark winter," the female voice said. "Veronica Masters from the Lasting Image Gallery. I love the work you sent me, Simon, particularly the ones with the parrot." When she said her name, I conjured an image of her tall slender frame, doe eyes, freckles and curly red hair.

"Don Verde is quite a subject. I'm glad you like them," I said.

"The art world needs to see these, and I'd like to mount an exhibition," Veronica said. "These are fabulous, Simon. The parrot is great. I'm thinking maybe twenty-four pieces—some more studies of Don Verde would be perfect."

"I think I can do that," I sputtered. "What time frame are we looking at?"

"How about next November?" She took a moment, probably leafing through her calendar. "The first Saturday in the month is the fifth. Let's shoot for the fifth for the opening."

"That's great, Veronica. I think that's lots of time for me to do a few more between now and then."

"How are you doing, anyway?" she asked. That didn't sound like business. As big as New York was, it was still a small town in some circles. She'd been at my last exhibition and probably knew all the grisly details.

"What can I say? A year has passed, a lot of legal fees, a lot of stress," I said, sighing. "But I have to say that I have certainly relaxed a lot since moving here."

"A divorce requires time to heal," she said. "It's like the amputation of a limb."

"You sound like you speak from experience."

"That I do, Simon. That I do. I was divorced five years ago, and it hasn't been easy, so I know there are good days and bad. But it sounds like the good ones are outnumbering the bad for you, and that's positive news."

"Thank you." I cleared my throat, and she coughed. Back to business.

"If you can ship the work up in early October, I can have them framed and hung."

"I think I'd like to come early and bring them with me. I have a place to stay, and I could supervise the framing and help hang the show. Do some publicity while I'm there."

"Sounds great, Simon. Keep in touch, and when you've done some more paintings, email the jpegs to me. This is exciting."

"Will do." And that was that. I had a show. I made a note on the calendar on the fridge, poured more coffee, and went out to sit on the veranda. Don Verde swooped in as if he'd been waiting for me.

"You are going to be a star, Don Verde. How do you like that?"

He responded immediately. "You're kidding. I don't believe it. You're kidding, right?"

He had the phrases down pat now and he sounded exactly like me.

16.

"THOSE FIREWORKS are driving me crazy." Coffee had just arrived, and Antonio was doctoring his with sugar. "Sometimes it sounds like a bunch of assault rifles; other times bombs or rocket missiles. I feel like we're back in the eighties, during the Nicaraguan revolution, and I should be running."

"If they did start a war during Purísima, the army would have to canvas people for gunpowder," Marco joked. He was watching the action across the street. It was early morning on the eighth of December; Antonio and Marco were waiting for their ham and eggs to arrive on the terrace restaurant of Hotel Alhambra in Granada. Across the street, on the edge of Parque Central, teams of drowsy horses were harnessed to carriages, their manes braided with ribbon rosettes. They stood at ease, like tired hookers, waiting for their next customers. Street cleaners methodically swept up manure and scrubbed puddles of urine over to the drains, their cleaning solution freshening the potentially fetid air.

"You couldn't tell a gunshot from a firecracker," Antonio remarked as he tucked into the plate set before him. "What a tradition."

At the time of the Conquest, the Spanish had introduced Catholicism and with it, Purísima, this annual holiday, which included massive amounts of gunpowder. The *indigenas* loved the event, as did their descendants, hundreds of years later. Households raised altars in their homes to honour the purity of the Virgin Mary and invited friends and family to spend the evening of December 7 together, before they went to church. The hosts provided a meal and gave their guests small gifts. Later that night, in churches all over Nicaragua, priests asked their congregations the question, "Who is the cause of all this happiness?" And in response, the parishioners screamed and yelled, "The Blessed Virgin Mary!" Fireworks continued to explode well beyond dawn, fuelled and fanned with drunken revelry. But the fireworks weren't exclusive to that night; they'd been blasting for more than a week. And now, the day after La Purísima, even though it was daylight, there was no sign of letting up.

"Most of the people that bought fireworks and cherry bombs to observe last night won't have money to buy tortillas this morning." Marco mopped up egg yolk with a piece of toast and popped it in his mouth. "Do you realize that one of those little cherry bombs cost one hundred córdobas? That would feed a family for a day with chicken, rice, and beans. *Dios mio*."

When they'd paid the bill, they headed to the bank. They'd spent all their cash on the hotel and breakfast. At the entrance to the bank, armed security guards flanked the glass doors, seemingly passive but for their guns. While they queued for the automatic teller machines, four uniformed men climbed the stairs from the basement, each carrying a large metal box the size of a drawer from a filing cabinet. Whatever they were toting wasn't light, for all men strained, waddling, with their arms fully extended and their knees bent. Outside, a truck idled, waiting for the men and their cargo.

"Hey, Marco. Have you ever had a safety deposit box?" Antonio asked.

"No, but my grandmother did. I often went with her when she needed documents or to put in or take out jewellery." Marco's turn in line came and he stuck his debit card into the ATM. He retrieved the cash and waited while Antonio made his transaction.

"How many were there?" Antonio asked when they were on the street again.

"How many what?"

"Safety deposit boxes."

"Hell, I don't know. Two long walls and one short one. Maybe a couple hundred."

"How big were they?"

"Long and narrow, and they probably came in small, medium, and large," Marco said. "My grandmother had a medium-sized one because I saw drawers that were smaller, and others that were larger than hers." The answer seemed to satisfy Antonio, and they remained silent as they started walking in the direction of the lake. Despite the punishing rays of the sun, when they walked on the shaded side of the street, the breeze felt cool, refreshing.

When they first met, Marco and Antonio had set a goal of making a million dollars together. It had taken them a few years, but the recent larger cocaine deals and Don Verde's short runs had pushed them over the top. Now, they were waiting for the marijuana harvest on Antonio's land near the border between Nicaragua and Honduras—a vast, secluded acreage from which they anticipated a large harvest.

They walked along the Malecón de la Amistad, swatting at clouds of midges that drifted on the breeze. They sat on the breakwater and watched the distant launches transport tourists through the archipelago beneath the shadow of the sleeping Mombacho volcano. The last time it erupted, it spewed more than three hundred islets onto the lake. Rich Nicaraguan families had built mansions on some of the larger islands; modest dwellings had been constructed on others, and there were some small islands with shacks and rickety fishing boats tied to makeshift docks. One was called Monkey Island, where monkeys had been introduced as a tourist attraction. Only a couple of mango trees grew there; otherwise, the animals depended on donations of bananas and other fruits from people on the tour boats.

"Have you ever dreamed of living on an island in a mansion like one of those?" Antonio was skipping stones across the water. Marco had befriended a horse that was grazing on the shoreline. He looked across at the islands.

"Not really. I've just left a house on the ocean. That dream is gone. I can't say I have any more."

"What do you mean, man? We're raking it in. How come you let it go?"

"Had to." Marco looked out at the herons. The water was shallow for quite a distance, and the birds were able to fish far beyond the shoreline. Isabella shimmered in the sunlight, wading among the herons, eyeing him with a coy smile. Marco shivered. "A lot of shit has gone down, Tonio. A lot. You would have read about it if you lived in Costa Rica."

"What's this all about, Marco?"

"If I'd stayed, I'd be up on a murder charge. Antonio, Isabella is dead. We fought, and she hit me with a vase. I ran at her, and she fell back and hit her head on our desk. When I realized she was dead, I got scared and hid her body in the well. The new owner of the house discovered her body a little while ago." He rubbed the horse's back vigorously, as if trying to remove a spot. His shoulders shook and tears welled in his eyes. "And even worse than her dying, Tonio, I have since learned she was going to have a baby. My baby." He collapsed against the horse; it remained calm, eating grass, while Marco's tears seeped into the animal's thirsty hide. Antonio approached him and laid his hand on his shoulder.

"I'm so sorry, man. I knew something was bothering you."

"Bothering me? It's eating me like gangrene."

"Give it time, Marco. You need time to heal. You're safe here."

"What's the good of money if you don't have someone to share it with? If I did have a dream, it would be to retire from this risky business, settle down, and raise a family with the woman I love. I've blown that."

"There'll be another opportunity, man. You're young, fairly good-looking, and somewhat well off."

"Yeah. Well. That doesn't seem so hopeful right now."

"Like I said, give it time."

17.

WHEN VERONICA MASTERS set the phone back on its charger, she turned to her computer, logged onto her calendar, and noted the dates for Simon Patrick's show. Then, she sent emails to the staff with the information. She crossed to the staff lounge and also wrote the information on the calendar fixed to the bulletin board, poured a mug of coffee, and sat at her desk. Once again, looking at the images he'd sent her, she remembered his last show, inspired by his trip to Africa years before: The gallery like a dimly lit jungle-scape, life-sized jungle cats stalking, playing and virtually jumping out of the spotlit canvases. There'd been a soundtrack of night sounds playing softly in the background: choruses of crickets and frogs, hyenas laughing, lions roaring, distant drums. The gallery had been overflowing with people, some on the street, waiting to enter. Simon was totally immersed in the people around him, oblivious to what was going on near the wine table. But while Simon chatted with prospective buyers, many others watched a mating dance.

Simon's wife Ingrid had cornered the willing Jeff Jaynes, gallery owner and host for the evening. One of the staff said Ingrid had twisted and rubbed against him like a cat in heat. At one point, she was practically on top of him. Well, before the gallery closed, she and Jeff had slipped out the back door. It had been awkward for the staff. One of them had to explain to Simon, stammering and stuttering, that Ingrid had gotten a ride with Jeff. None the wiser—no doubt, still revved from the success of his show—Simon had hailed a cab and gone home alone to an empty house. It wasn't until the following morning, when he arrived at the gallery to get his cheque, that he learned what had happened, or at least a version of it. Rumours had infected the art community like a virus, and one truth among several falsehoods was Simon's divorce. Memories of her own separation and divorce resurfaced when she thought about his. Fortunately, the pain, anger, and humiliation she'd suffered, she felt no longer.

And from the look of his vibrant work and the sound of his voice, Simon didn't seem to harbour those feelings any longer either. They had both moved on.

18.

"AMAZING THAT WE'RE only twenty minutes out of Granada, and the air is so much cooler," Marco said. His arm was out the window, his hand dipping and soaring with the air current. Antonio was driving up the highway to the village of Catarina, in the mountains overlooking Laguna de Apoyo. Marco had been complaining about the heat in Granada since he'd arrived, and though Antonio was accustomed to it, he agreed that he'd like to get out of the city. It would be quieter. There would doubtless be fireworks, but the population of Catarina was a small fraction compared to Granada, and perhaps the residents didn't spend all their money on pyrotechnics.

They parked in the lot near the square and walked up to the *mirador* to sit on a bench and look out at the view. But there was nothing to see; they were enveloped in fog.

"I'm no scientist, but since the air up here is so much cooler, when it meets with the warm water of Laguna de Apoyo, fog rises," Marco said. Antonio didn't respond. He was already standing, ready to go. "Wait. Relax," Marco said.

Antonio strode to the railing and back. He rattled his keys before tossing them in the air. And then the light began to change.

"Look at that," Marco said. "What did I tell you?" The fog started to dissipate, and the lake gradually appeared below them, like a mirage, wisps of cloud drifting in the sunlight.

"This place is magical. Laguna de Apoyo—maybe it will live up to its name and offer us aid and support."

They'd rented the top floor of a five-storey apartment building. Their terrace covered half the roof beyond their patio doors, and Marco had visited several local *viveros* and selected plants and trees to create a rooftop garden: Four potted lipstick palms separated the open sunning area from the shaded patio that he had created by draping lengths of white canvas over a frame attached to the outside wall of the building. Bougainvillea and lantana grew in pots along with lilies, hibiscus, and roses.

Marco continued to go to church and sensed a change. Something was happening; he was starting to feel calmer, at ease. Maybe God was listening. He continued to light three candles each day, and each day he prayed longer, found himself staying longer, until one Sunday, he decided to attend mass. The priest was down-to-earth; the message of his sermon was judgement, and Marco felt as if it were directed at him personally. On the way down the steps, he wasn't paying attention and bumped into a beautiful woman. He apologized. She smiled and told him not to worry. He invited her for coffee. Her name was Sylvia Mendoza.

"I haven't seen you here before," Sylvia remarked when they sat down and had coffee brought to them.

"My buddy and I are renting the top floor of that apartment building over there," Marco said, pointing to the west. "We moved up here from Granada. Well, actually I'm Costa Rican, originally from San José. I'm babbling; forgive me. Do you live right in Catarina?"

"I'm a seamstress and have a shop in the front room of the house I rent. I moved here about a year ago. I'm from Rivas."

When he learned that she loved plants and flowers, he suggested they go to a *vivero* down the road. She pointed out her house when they walked by. The lights were on, and a woman was measuring a customer.

"That's Lidia. She opened up this morning and will leave early when I get back. Then I will close up. It's a great arrangement; not like being a prisoner to your business. She also shares my house." When they reached the *vivero,* she grinned like a child about to enter a candy shop. She had a bubbly personality; her laughter sounded like a brook tumbling over smooth stones. He held the gate open for her, and she headed straight for the jasmine shrubs, her nose into them like a bloodhound on a trail. She selected a mid-sized bush that was covered with blossoms, some of which had opened. She continued inhaling their fragrance. Marco chose a larger one with fewer blooms. He refused to let her pay.

"My treat," he said, slipping inside the building. He gave a handful of córdobas to the owner and walked outside to join Sylvia. She was still enjoying the fragrance of the blossoms. He hadn't noticed before but now, the way she held the plant up to her face, he saw angry-looking ropes of purple scars on her bare arm and neck. He said nothing. He walked her back to her shop where she set the plant at the front entrance.

"Thanks again for the jasmine," she said.

"You're more than welcome. Perhaps we could have dinner some time," Marco suggested. Her smile was framed, beaming from the doorway.

"I would like that," she replied. As she closed the door, the chimes attached to it tinkled in what Marco thought was a cheerful, welcoming sound. Perhaps it augured well—anyway, it was better than the sound of a slamming door. He continued on to his apartment.

Antonio wasn't home, but he had left evidence that he'd been sitting outside before he left: a couple of cigarette butts in the ashtray and an empty coffee mug that had left dried brown rings on the table.

He set the jasmine at the edge of the patio where the fragrance would drift when the flowers opened. Sylvia drifted back into his mind as well. He made fresh coffee, and after removing

Antonio's detritus, sat down at the glass table. Maybe he could make Christmas dinner for Sylvia and her friend. Why not? He'd invite her out to dinner and then suggest it. Or maybe she spent Christmas with her family. No harm in asking, though.

19.

THE DOOR CHIMES jingled when Sylvia Mendoza closed the door, still smiling from Marco's invitation to dinner. The whole encounter, actually. When they bumped into each other, she felt like she had been pushed into him. Her face blazed, and she breathed deeply before she turned from the door and walked into the room. Lidia looked up from the trousers she was hemming.

"What happened to you? You get that worked up from going to mass? Did the priest come onto you?"

Sylvia chuckled. "No, no. I met a guy at church, and he invited me to have coffee with him. Then we went to a *vivero*. He bought me a jasmine. It's outside."

"Well, well." Thankfully, Lidia said nothing more and continued working. Sylvia stuffed her handbag under the counter and went back out the door. She picked up the potted jasmine and breathed in its intoxicating fragrance. Marco Alvarez Soto. He seemed like a nice guy. The first man to buy her flowers; the first man she'd spent any time with since she left her husband a year ago. It had taken a whole year to extinguish all the rage she'd felt, a year for scars to fade on her wounds—on her body and in her heart. The divorce had been rapid, unequivocal. She'd not had to see the man who had slashed her, broke her ribs, and blackened her eyes. She'd endured, indeed, suffered through her marriage, believing his blubbery apologies. Perhaps the previous assaults on her hadn't been serious enough for her to go to the doctor, but when he slashed her, she knew the cuts were deep and long. He'd been so drunk, he didn't see her crawl out of the house to ask a neighbour to take her to Emergency. The only time she'd gone back was after she was sure he was at work. Then, she and a girlfriend had gone in, packed her things, and left her key on the table. She had taken a bus to Granada and another up to Catarina.

She knew she'd made the right decision when she met a woman on the bus and learned that the woman had also fled an abusive relationship. She was living in a hostel and took Sylvia there when they arrived in Catarina. Sylvia could afford to rent a house and began looking for a place large enough for the other woman and herself, with a room that could be used for sewing, doing alterations and repairs. That was a year ago, and during that time, two other women had arrived on her doorstep; Lidia was the most recent. Together, they healed; they talked and laughed and cried. They got perspective on their lives, or at least, Sylvia had. She was still wary, like the rest of the women, but she felt more open and perhaps what happened today was an indication that the healing was complete.

20.

I STARTED RESEARCHING parrots on the internet—learned that there are more than three hundred and fifty species in the world. Far as I could tell, Don Verde appeared to be an *Amazona auropalliata,* or yellow-naped parrot. He had a red diamond-shaped marking of feathers on his head, unlike others I saw online, but I learned that this was his own individual characteristic. Others had stripes of feathers that looked like moustaches, while others had splashes of colour on their backs or wings. It made them recognizable, easily picked out of a flock. I was interested in their wing and feather structure. Don Verde sauntered back and forth on the table by my easel, providing me with close-up views of his form. He had four claws on each foot—two facing forward and two back—which allowed him to climb, to put food in his mouth, and to scratch. I tried to find anything about their ability to fly distances, and though there was some information about migratory parrots, no one seemed to know how far or if they had homing instincts like pigeons. But I didn't need that kind of information to paint; I was just curious.

On New Year's Day, Don Verde followed me down to the beach, occasionally landing on my shoulder when he wanted to rest, then flying off ahead of me. We came back and ate nuts and mangoes together. I had coffee and he sipped water and chuckled like me. I returned to the easel and what I'd started on New Year's Eve: *Don Verde on Parade*, like he did when he marched back and forth on the table. I was starting to fill in some of his flight feathers when the phone rang.

"Simon Patrick," Don Verde said as soon as I picked up the phone.

"Happy New Year, Simon," Veronica said.

"Actually, that wasn't me speaking. It was Don Verde."

"You're kidding."

"He says that, too. Exactly like me. Soon, I can stop talking altogether."

"I don't believe it."

"That's another one of his expressions—or mine that he's copied. Anyway, thank you, and happy New Year to you, too."

"So did you go out and celebrate last night?"

"I made it as far as the shoreline, witnessed a meteor shower, made a wish, and stayed out on the veranda. If you can call that going out, then I did. What about you?"

"I lit a fire, opened a bottle of Merlot, and curled up with a Robert Wilson novel."

"I've only read one of his: *A Small Death in Lisbon*."

"That's the one I'm reading. Great book. Don't know how I hadn't heard of him before."

"So, each of us entertained ourselves privately on one of—no, *the*—most celebrated nights of the year. Did you make any resolutions?"

"Two so far, and the day isn't over yet. One is to get out of this deep-freeze, and another is to travel. Both would be preventative medicines to combat winter depression, an insidious malaise that's got everyone and the economy in its grips. People are down and don't want to spend. Not on art, at least. Perhaps they think their money is better spent on cozy sweaters and eiderdown duvets. Believe me, we could all use some of the natural vitamin D like you're getting."

"I have a guest room. You're welcome to come down here for that dose of vitamin D."

"I couldn't impose, Simon. You're working ... and it's for me you're working. I don't want to upset your routine."

"I'd let you know if you upset my routine. Think about it for a while and let me know."

"That's very kind of you, Simon. Thank you. I will."

She called the following afternoon from the gallery.

"Me again. My staff gave me the green light to get away for a while. Business is slow, and there aren't any shows until next month. Nothing they can't take care of. In fact, I think they are relieved I'm going; I've been kind of grumpy."

"So when are you thinking about coming?"

"There's a flight this Friday afternoon that I can make if there's still a seat."

"Great." I hoped she couldn't hear me gulp. "Send me the details when you get them, and I'll be at the airport to collect you."

21.

ANTONIO VARGAS PARKED his Mercedes in the open area outside Claro Americas Cable Company and walked along the cobblestone street. Nearby, outside a café, two old gringos were getting revved up on coffee, their opinions boiling over and infecting the quiet morning. It was early; vendors were setting up their wares along the north side of Parque Central. Carriages queued along the west side of the park, patient horses sleeping. He walked down Calle La Calzada and sat at a table outside Café de los Sueños. The owner, a young French Canadian, greeted him and placed a menu in front of him.

"Good morning André. I don't need a menu. Just bring me a coffee and a panino with ham and cheese. Please," he added. André bowed, took the menu, and disappeared inside. Antonio sat back and surveyed the street. Some restaurants and bars were still closed while staff of the various establishments swept the insidious dust off their patios, then hosed them down for the first of what would probably be many times during the day. A man with a sandy-grey ponytail sticking out from under his baseball cap sat down at the table next to him.

"Mornin'," the man said. Though he had uttered only one word, Antonio was sure he was an American. Maybe it was the inflection or his body language.

"Good morning," Antonio answered. He smiled and sipped his coffee.

"Got a light?" the man asked.

Antonio fished a lighter out of his pocket and handed it to him.

"Thanks. Where you from?"

"I was born here in Granada," Antonio said.

"No shit."

"What about you?" Antonio asked, trying to be polite.

"I'm originally from Cleveland, Ohio, but I've rented a little house on Calle El Arsenal for a few months," the man said, handing back the lighter. "My landlord is a buddy, an ex-Marine like myself. He rents the place out when he travels. Some kind of consulting work." The owner arrived with Antonio's panino and handed a menu to the new man. "What he's having looks good. I'll have the same." He turned back to Antonio. "Why don't you join me?" He stood and extended his hand to Antonio. "Nick Bacon. Pleased to meet you, man."

"Antonio Vargas. Likewise." Antonio shook Nick's hand, pulled out one of the chairs opposite him and then set his panino on the table in front of him.

"You go ahead and eat, Antonio. Etiquette ain't worth shit when you're hungry." Antonio smiled, took a bite, and remained quiet until he swallowed.

"Where was your tour of duty, Nick?" Antonio was thinking about his great-uncle Augusto Sandino, and how he and his men had thumped the Marines.

"First Afghanistan. Then Iraq. I was there for three years. Had enough." In-between mouthfuls of their panini, Antonio learned that Nick was an explosives expert. That he'd built plastic bombs during his time in the Marines. In turn, Antonio told him that he was in the exporting business.

"Did a bit of that in my time, too." Nick said, and chuckled. "You look cool to me, so I don't mind telling you that I brought a lot of carpets back from the Middle East with opium rolled inside them." So, he was a U.S. Marine who was into dealing, Antonio thought, then wondered what other kinds of nefarious acts Nick had been involved in. Antonio grinned amiably, nodding at Nick's declaration. They finished their breakfast and continued to talk, ordered more and more coffee, interspersed with trips to the men's room inside the restaurant. The sun was almost overhead, and André came out to raise the umbrellas.

"You guys alright here?" he asked. He'd unfurled their umbrella and was moving on to the next table.

"Actually, I think it's about time for a beer," Nick said. "What do you think, Antonio?"

"Sure. I'll have a beer," Antonio said as André took the full ashtray and set down a clean one. "Two Toñas, please."

The beer order seemed to relax both of them. They clinked their bottles, wished each other good health, and swilled ice-cold brew for another couple of hours. Antonio was interested in Nick's knowledge of explosives.

"No more TNT in a box with a plunger," he said. "That only happens in cartoons and old ones at that," Nick told him. "When the explosives are all set in place, they can be detonated by a cellphone. Easy as pressing a number. Hell, with a cellphone, a computer and a GPS, you could blow up a continent."

"Interesting." Antonio's mind was active, absorbing the information.

"You should come by the house some day, and I'll show you a simulation program I designed for the troops, sort of an orientation kind of thing. I shouldn't have it, but what Uncle Sam don't know, won't hurt him." Nick laughed, finished his beer, and signalled to the waiter for their bill.

"I'd like that, Nick. I'll be back in town in a couple of days." They exchanged numbers, and Antonio noted Nick's address. "I know where that is," he said. "I used to live near there."

"Great then. Look forward to hearing from you."

22.

NICK BACON HAD no trouble sleeping. He was an expert catnapper, thanks to his time in the Marines, when he caught winks wherever and whenever possible. And when he lay his head on his own pillow, in his own bed, his sleep was normally deep and uninterrupted until eight hours later when he awoke refreshed and ready for the day.

The night after he'd met Antonio, Nick had gone to bed as usual and fell asleep quickly. He heard the *clip-clop* of tired horses, iron-edged wheels clattering on the cobblestone street. He went to the front door and opened the peephole. Coming up the street was a cart led by two horses and driven by someone with a black hood covering his shoulders and head. As the cart approached, Nick gasped, horrified. Beneath the hood, Nick saw bright eyes illuminating a skeletal face. He jerked away from the door and awakened to find himself in the living room at the front door. The peephole was open, and he heard a deep sonorous voice coming from outside. The voice was speaking English, but the Spanish accent was so thick that Nick couldn't understand much except the man's name: Consolación. He thought he was trying to encourage Nick to go with him to a place called La Libertad. Consolación's hand reached through the peephole and grabbed Nick's shoulder. He woke up. He was in bed, tangled in his sheets, like a mummy. He went to the front door. The peephole was closed and locked from the inside.

23.

AS SOON AS I'd hung up, I felt claustrophobic, and I had only a few days to get over it. Veronica was coming at the end of the week. What had I done? I'd just gotten used to being alone. I was feeling creative again, happy in my skin. Was I going to let this woman get under it? Luckily, I'd finished painting for the day, otherwise I would have been too distracted to concentrate. I poured another mug of coffee and carried it with me down to the beach where the sound of the waves crashing against the shore kept my attention. This was foolish. I was being selfish and silly. She was responsible for my future, my re-entry into the art scene in New York. She was a professional woman, there was lots of room here, and I had said that I would let her know if she was disturbing my routine. I would, dammit.

Maria came during the middle of the week, and I asked her to get the guest room ready, informing her I would be having a guest, a woman. Maria's dark skin turned even darker. She smiled and went about cleaning the house. While Maria was cleaning, I drove to town and bought groceries, and when I'd put them away I surveyed the house. It sparkled. The guest room was fresh and spotless, with a bouquet of lilies centred in a vase on the bureau. I'd arranged some of my paintings on small easels; the rest were in a box, and my friend Don Verde was keeping an eye on things outside.

Early Friday morning, I drove to the Liberia International

Airport at the north end of the city. The flowering trees and shrubs were a riot of colour along the drive. I had finally relaxed and was looking forward to seeing her.

The flight from New York was fully booked with pale, pasty-looking winter refugees seeking asylum from their frigid nightmares, if only for two weeks. Veronica towered above the other passengers, many of them wider than they were tall, amplified by loud colourful outfits. Veronica cleared Immigration, and once she'd collected her checked baggage, she appeared at the gate where we all waited for the emerging passengers. She smiled and waved when she recognized me.

"Hi Veronica. Welcome to Costa Rica." I extended my hand, shook hers, pecked her on the cheek, and reached for her bag. "How was the trip?"

"Uneventful, thank God. Oh, it's so great to be here." She stood by the car with her arms extended and her face heavenward. "Look at this colour: the flowers and the vibrant shades of green. No wonder you're inspired here."

"I'm definitely moved around by the place, and as they say, 'you ain't seen nothin' yet.'"

I drove to my favourite restaurant at a hotel on the ocean. When I parked the car, Veronica was out in a flash, sprinting for the sand beyond the restaurant, already barefoot. She unbuttoned her blouse and shed it down to a lilac-coloured teddy. She rolled up her pant legs and walked in the shallow water at the shore's edge. I ordered two bottles of Pilsen, my favourite Costa Rican beer and sat at a table at the furthest edge of the restaurant, near the sand. When she was sufficiently cooled and able to sit down, she sighed and smiled at me.

"This is exactly what the doctor ordered," she declared. She looked at the shoreline. "Do you live near here?"

"About a half-hour's walk, or a ten-minute drive to the north," I said. We were perusing the menu. I ordered steak. She had shrimp. We chattered while waiting for our meals to arrive, and when they did, we continued talking between mouthfuls.

A couple of times we acted like a couple who'd been together a long time, picking from each other's plates, never missing a beat. Our conversation ranged from local culture to the weather, from my property to my work.

"How is your painting going, Simon?"

"I can't tell, really. I think it's good, but you'll have to judge for yourself."

"Can't wait." Coffee had arrived, and she doctored hers with sugar. "Tell me what your daily routine is—when you like to work. As I said, I don't want to intrude on your life, and I can amuse myself."

24.

SYLVIA ACCEPTED Marco's invitation to dinner. He picked her up, and they drove down to Granada in his new BMW SUV. Calle La Calzada was decorated for Christmas. North of the cathedral, on the square, a thirty-foot tree twinkled with hundreds of lights the colours of the rainbow. Before they went to dinner, they entered the church where they both lit candles and made their private supplications.

Marco had made reservations at the Mona Lisa, a restaurant specializing in pizza and Italian food. They made their own pasta and prepared an excellent Caesar salad like a scene from an Italian version of *Babette's Feast*.

Marco and Sylvia sat at a table outside. When she reached across the table for the breadbasket, Marco once again noticed the angry scars on her arm. "May I ask what happened to your arm, Sylvia?"

Her smiling expression didn't change nor did she hesitate. "Of course." She took the bread and offered him some. "My husband did it. He was drunk; we were fighting. He dropped a liquor bottle and when it broke and spilled his precious elixir, he took it out on me. Again." She buttered the bread and nibbled at a corner of it. "It's a lasting reminder. Bruises fade and are easily forgotten. Scars remain. That's why I'm here. I laid charges when I was still in the hospital. Then I filed for divorce and left." She twirled her pasta on her fork, looked at him again.

"Do you have any children?" he asked. She looked beyond him to the lake that she could not see.

"No. I wanted to. But not with him," she said. "What about you? Have you been married?" she asked.

Marco gulped, almost choked on his wine. "Yes." It was almost a whisper. "But she died," he added.

Sylvia wondered if Marco's wife had been a cancer victim. "Oh. I'm so sorry, Marco." She reached over to touch his hand. "Any children?"

"No. But she was two months pregnant when she died." He didn't know where to look.

"Oh, Marco. I'm so sorry," she said, her hands reaching for his. She didn't ask any more questions and Marco didn't offer any more information. They were quiet in their thoughts, finishing their pasta.

"When I first came here, I thought that Laguna de Apoyo might live up to its name and offer me some support," Marco confessed. "Maybe it is doing just that. We have both come here to recover. For some reason, we bumped into each other—literally!" They both laughed at the recollection. "Maybe the lake *is* offering its aid and support."

Sylvia nodded and looked at him, he thought, in a different way. She smiled encouragingly.

"Do you have plans for Christmas?" he asked. He poured the last of the wine into their glasses. "Do you get together with family?"

"My parents are no longer living. My brother is in Venezuela and my sister is in Los Angeles, so it's virtually impossible—too costly—for us all to get together. Lidia doesn't have any family near here, either—she too escaped a violent husband." She laughed. "I've had a few women stay with me in the past year. Sometimes, I think I should start a shelter for battered women."

Marco's throat was constricting again. He sipped his wine, swallowed. "Why don't you both come for dinner on Christmas Eve? I'm a fairly good cook, and I'd love to make dinner for you both. And my buddy Antonio will be there, of course. We're all Christmas orphans," he said.

25.

VERONICA WAS THE PERFECT house guest. I never told her my routine; she simply seemed to intuit and go with the flow. In the mornings, we had coffee together and took walks along the beach. When we returned, and I started making motions to start painting, she grabbed a book, a blanket, and an umbrella and went down to the beach. Don Verde divided his time between his perch on my easel and Veronica's chair. When she returned at midday, she made lunch for us. I wasn't accustomed to such culinary treats: grilled fish with salad and rice, shrimp and pasta, and fabulous salads. She made good use of my garden and even did a little weeding.

After dinner one night, we were having a glass of wine on the veranda, and I remembered the wood I'd piled in the shed after I'd pruned the trees.

"How about a bonfire on the beach?" I got up, and she followed me to the shed. We loaded up with arms full of dried branches and logs. While I lit the fire, she went back to the house and returned with a blanket and beer. The branches were dry and caught the flame quickly. She laid the blanket a safe distance from potentially errant sparks, sat down, and uncapped the beer. I sat down beside her and she handed me one.

"Thanks." We clinked bottles. "This is another first for me here. My first bonfire on the beach. In fact, you're my first house guest, too."

"You can't imagine how much I appreciate being here, Simon. It's truly a gift." The flames from the fire illuminated her contented smile, set her curls afire.

"It's good to have you here," I admitted. "I have to confess that after I offered, I got anxious, like I was feeling claustrophobic, but that is totally gone now."

"I'm certainly glad. I wouldn't want to make you feel uncomfortable in your own home—especially when you're working for me. That would be terrible."

I put my arm over her shoulder in a friendly gesture. She leaned into it and rested her head against my chest. We remained silent and both stared at the fire, thoughts drifting on the breeze.

"I feel like I've been riding on a noisy, vibrating motorcycle for thousands of miles, across deserts, over rough roads and riverbeds. I have reached my destination, my oasis, and for the first few hours, I continued to vibrate, like I was still on that motorcycle." She looked up at me and smiled. "I've finally slowed down."

"I remember feeling like that when I first got here. The buzz of New York was still in my ears. It's good to know that we're able to function at both speeds and can change gears—if we have to." I poked at the dying embers with the one remaining stick.

"I've saved enough wood for a couple more fires. Maybe we should let this one die down and have another one tomorrow night." We sat for a few more minutes watching the embers glow. She shook out the blanket and gathered up the empty bottles, and I threw sand on the fire. On the walk back to the house, my arm found its way over her shoulder again. This time, she slipped her arm across my back, rested her head on my shoulder. On the veranda, my hurricane lamps flickered a welcoming golden light. When we reached the bottom step, we both hesitated, and as if choreographed, turned to face each other. She raised her head and looked into my eyes. We kissed. That's all I can say, not who initiated it, for our lips met simultaneously, like they were on some preordained course. Tender and lingering, pleasant. And that's all that happened.

We climbed the steps, said good night, and prepared for bed.

But I couldn't sleep, thinking about our gentle encounter, how comfortable and easy. I chastised myself. She lived in New York, the place I had fled. I was happy here. I couldn't get involved. I tossed and turned until just before dawn, but thankfully fell asleep before the birds started singing or I wouldn't have slept at all.

Veronica had the coffee made and was sitting on the veranda when I finally got up. She was reading, but smiled at me when I opened the door. She set her book down. "Good morning," she said. "Did you sleep well?"

"To tell you the truth, no. Not really." I sat down in the other rocking chair. She poured me a mug of coffee from the carafe on the table. "Thanks." I took a sip and thought for a moment. "And to continue in honesty, our kiss was the first physical contact I've had with anyone since Ingrid. Kind of moved me around. How about yourself? How did you sleep?"

"When I did get to sleep, I slept fine." The leather seat squeaked as she tried to tuck her legs underneath her on the chair. "I have to confess that I haven't kissed anyone in a long time either, Simon." She looked into her coffee and then grinned. "But I'm very proud of the way we restrained ourselves, even though it was difficult to settle down afterwards."

"I can't believe we're having this conversation," I said and laughed. I was echoed; Don Verde had been listening. "I can't believe it, VER-ON-I-CA," he said.

The following night, we carried more wood down for a bonfire but before I'd put a match to it, Veronica called me to the shoreline.

"Look, Simon. A leatherback turtle! She's coming ashore to lay her eggs."

We watched a monstrous turtle wash in on a wave and begin her trek. She was like an aquatic sand plow; her long front flippers edged her up past the tide line, which left tracks that would drift, change, and disappear with the offshore breezes.

"She's going up to the treeline," Veronica whispered, though there was no need.

"How do you know?"

"I studied marine biology at Boston U. I aspired to be a female Jacques Cousteau."

"What happened with that?"

"I went to an art exhibit, fell in love with painting, and switched courses."

She was walking slowly in the turtle's direction. "She may have laid her eggs here before and knows exactly where she's going."

We stayed a safe distance away from her and watched as she dug down into the sand, in what appeared to be an extremely laborious effort, her flippers not the most sophisticated excavating tools. Veronica watched, fascinated. I could almost see her conjuring up the information she'd learned about this enormous creature.

"How many eggs does she lay, and how long does it take them to hatch?" I asked.

"In one sitting, she can lay more than a hundred eggs in a clutch, but she could have as many as seven clutches in safe areas where there is low predation. However, only about eighty-five percent of those eggs might be viable. Takes about two months for the eggs to hatch. The mortality rate is high, though. As eggs and then as hatchlings, they are very vulnerable to predators. But if they make it to adulthood, they have few predators. I read an account of a shark trying to bite a leatherback and the turtle chased the shark before it attacked the boat in which people had been witnessing the chase."

The turtle was covering the clutch of eggs she'd laid; her flippers looked so cumbersome, but Veronica said the long flippers made them incredibly fast swimmers. "In about two months time, keep your eye out in the evenings, and you may see the hatchlings head for the sea. Wish I could be here."

26.

ANTONIO SLID A CHAIR across the floor, next to Nick Bacon's, who was sitting at his computer. His little house on Calle El Arsenal was beautifully restored, but it was probably a fraction in size of the original house, which would have had a central garden as well as corridors leading off in all directions to other rooms. The residences on either side of Nick's would have comprised the entire hacienda. The Caña de India strapped ceilings looked to be twelve feet high, or more, with transoms over the huge double doors that divided the living room from the rest of the house. Carved grates above the street-side double doors had been the ingenious ventilation system of the era, but now they were glassed in, adapted for air conditioning. On the white stucco walls and draped over his sofa and chairs were some of the exquisite carpets he'd brought from his tour of the Middle East. No sign of the opium though.

"This is the simulation program I was telling you about." Nick was clicking on an icon on his screen. A map appeared. "The areas where the bombs have been planted are marked in red, all located by GPS. You click on the bomb you want to detonate and a drop-down menu appears, asking for confirmation. Click on 'yes,' click on 'detonate,' and *kaboom!* Here, you try it."

Antonio gripped the mouse and repeated all the steps that Nick had taken. One of the blasts seemed to implode. "That one was placed underground, right?"

"Right. When we could get underground, we did. Otherwise, we stuck them to walls, bridges, roads."

Antonio had been visiting Nick on and off for about a month and had grown to like him. He'd been throwing hypothetical situations at him, trying to understand explosives and what was needed, and now it was time to level with him, tell him the plan. It would cost. He'd have to be partnered in, but it would be worth it. Nick's expertise was invaluable and would save them a lot of time and effort, he thought. He hoped.

"Ever heard of William Walker?" Antonio asked.

"A bit. Not a lot. Seen a sign somewhere near here. Before I came down, I read about him in guidebooks, and his part in the history of Nicaragua. Originally from Tennessee, right? He went to Costa Rica too, didn't he?"

"Oh yes. He stirred up a lot of turmoil in Mexico and Central America. In a rigged election, he declared himself president of Nicaragua in 1856, claiming to bring about democracy—his own brand—that reintroduced slavery and made the official language English. He only lasted a year. He burned the city down before he left, though, all but his house. He was finally executed in Honduras," Antonio explained, then suddenly jumped up. "You know, I'd like to show you something. Grab your keys, and let's step outside for a minute. Won't take long."

Nick swiped the keys off his desk, and they went out on the street. When Nick had locked the door, Antonio motioned up the street. "It's down this way. Not far." They walked west along Calle El Arsenal, and at the first intersecting block, he pointed at the San Francisco Convent.

"That's where Walker lived."

"I've heard it's the oldest building in Granada."

"That's because he ordered the rest of the city to be torched. Let's go back." When they were back inside, Antonio followed Nick to the fridge. He handed a bottle of beer to Antonio; they clinked bottles, settled around the kitchen table, and Antonio resumed his story.

"I lived with my grandmother in Masaya for a few years when I was a kid and she told me many stories." Antonio longed to tell him about his ancestor Augusto Sandino but remained focused. "William Walker was president of Nicaragua but his sinister activities in that short period of time are legend. *Abuela* told me that his slaves' quarters were in the cellar of that building. It was dark and virtually airless, and they probably lived among spiders and scorpions. Hideous kind of life." Both men were silent in their thoughts. Antonio cleared his throat and continued.

"*Abuela* says the slaves worked hard for Walker, but also for themselves. When they were dismissed for the night, bone-weary from working all day, they picked and dug and pawed at the dirt in that cellar, little by little, taking turns, spelling each other off to get some rest, and in that year they'd dug a tunnel heading to the lake. But Walker's slaves weren't the only ones. Likewise, in cellars under other houses, other slaves were doing the same thing, digging their Underground Railroad. Of course, they never made it. Before Walker fled, he had some of them shot, and others died in the conflagration. But my grandmother said that the tunnels still exist. Don't know how far they go, but I'd sure like to find out."

The next time Antonio visited Nick, he brought a map of the city of Granada. He laid it out on the dining-room table and reviewed what he'd learned. "I've marked the major banks' locations, one of which is very near the vicinity of these tunnels."

"You don't say." Nick leaned over the map, noting the markings. "We should be able to find a geological survey of the area to see what the soil is like. Not that we need it if the tunnels are close to each other. I'll bring up a map on my computer anyway, and we can feed information onto it, as you get it." Nick winked and turned back to his computer.

"My New Year's Resolution this year was to open bank accounts in all of the banks on that street," Antonio declared, indicating the boxes he'd drawn in red on the map. "Then,

I'll rent safety deposit boxes and start sussing out the logistics in the bowels of these institutions, particularly Banco LAFISE Bancentro." He pointed to one red dot further along Calle El Arsenal. "I'm not in a rush. I don't really need the money. I'm set. But I like the challenge of getting my head around a problem. I want to do it right and then I'll retire."

27.

WHEN SYLVIA AND LIDIA arrived at Marco and Antonio's for dinner on Christmas Eve, the blend of aromas coming from the kitchen drew them like butterflies to flowers. Marco had been up since dawn, making dressing, stuffing the turkey, peeling vegetables, and preparing his mother's chocoflan recipe. They arrived at six o'clock, when the last rays of sunlight had faded into dusk. The patio was lit with candles and hurricane lamps, which cast a warm light. The fragrance of the jasmine wafted on a gentle breeze. A small fire radiated heat from the *chimenea* near the table, just enough to take the chill off. The women looked beautiful. Their dresses were no doubt their own creations, complimented with shawls of soft wool that accented the colours in their dresses.

Antonio had been gracious, as usual, self-assured without being arrogant. Marco almost wished he were a woman, to enjoy this amicable side of his friend. What Antonio didn't know was the women's backgrounds of abuse. Marco hadn't told him, and he wouldn't know what was running through their minds while Antonio regaled them with his adventures—the legal ones. What were they thinking? They probably didn't trust men; how could they? Wariness would be policy. Marco felt fortunate to have been accepted by Sylvia, but he had only just met Lidia and didn't know her or how she might feel about things. She seemed friendly enough. They'd lingered around the table long after dessert and coffee, and then both women had insisted on helping to wash the dishes. They did them together—all except Antonio, who stoked the fire, smoked cigarettes, and drank more wine. When they'd tidied the kitchen and the women refused anything more to drink, Marco walked them home. They walked down the middle of the empty streets, Marco flanked by two beautiful women. They both had their arms through his, and once or twice, he thought he felt Sylvia squeeze his arm.

He opened the gate at Sylvia's house and moved aside to let them walk through, then shut it behind him. He walked them to the door. Lidia had the keys out of her purse and was aiming one of them at the lock. When she'd engaged the key, she turned. "It was very kind of you to invite me for dinner, Marco. Thank you, and have a Merry Christmas. Good night." She smiled at him and walked into the house.

"Yes, Marco. It was a lovely meal, and as Lidia says, so kind of you to invite us."

"It was my pleasure." Marco smiled and bowed a little. "Will you be going to mass tomorrow?"

"Yes."

"Then perhaps I'll see you in church. Merry Christmas, Sylvia." He kissed her on the cheek.

"Merry Christmas, Marco."

Marco was pleased with the evening. They were lovely women, and as the New Year approached, he was hatching a plan that would benefit them all.

28.

ANTONIO PARKED HIS MERCEDES in a shed by the shack where his workers slept during harvest time. He moved his ATV out, climbed on, and drove slowly along the path that led to the fields. The plantation was a secluded parcel of land between Somotillo and Villa Nueva, edged by a thick tangle of trees and vines. Beyond lay acres of tended fields, once pasture, and now the site for a healthy crop of robust flowering marijuana plants. When they hacked the plants down with their machetes, the workers had looked like little boys cutting down trees. They'd harvested last week, and now, row upon row of twine laced across the fields in a clever cat's cradle, upon which branches of bud dried, strung like garments on a clothesline. Swaths of plastic tarpaulin lay on the ground, and the men were clipping buds from the stocks. *Snip, plop, snip plop*; piles of fragrant flowers created mounds on the tarps.

Antonio had driven up from Léon where he'd stayed the night, the first time he'd entered the city since he'd fled from Señor Gómez decades before. He'd driven to the architect's house, where there seemed to be a party in progress. He stopped the car and peered through the open window. A young waiter dressed in black trousers and a stark white shirt was passing a tray of drinks to guests in the living room. Antonio gritted his teeth, remembering how stupid, how naïve he'd been. He wondered who the rich architect had in his clutches now. Perhaps the waiter did double duty. He put the car in gear and floored the gas pedal. The tires squealed and the smell of burning rubber was all he left behind.

He stood next to the truck with the driver who was eating a taco. The lights from the truck and Antonio's ATV lit their end of the field. Beyond, torches and flashlights augmented the slice of moon hanging above the treetops. They watched while one man sat atop the shipping container, receiving bundled tarps of clipped bud, dropping them into the hold, pushing it into the corners, tamping it down. They'd emptied a quarter of the lines that had laced the fields. Antonio lit a cigarette and offered one to the driver who'd finished his meal. He took the last drink of his Coke, crushed the can in his fist, tossed it, and accepted the smoke. When he threw the can, he almost hit one of the workers who was walking over to them, his face locked in a terrified grimace.

"Sorry, man. Didn't see you there," the driver shouted. The man didn't respond, continued walking towards them. His pants were stained down the front and his hands were shaking, rattling the straw hat with which he tried to cover his soiled trousers. He opened his mouth as if he were going to say something, then collapsed on the ground in front of them. Both men knelt to help him, loosened his shirt from his neck. The driver jumped in the cab of his truck and retrieved a bottle of Flor de Caña. He tilted the man's head and poured some of the rum into his mouth; he sputtered, coughed, and struggled to sit up. He swallowed some more rum before he spoke.

"I saw … I saw…. There's something in the field," he whispered, barely audible. "I'm finished, *jefe*. I won't go back out there." He stood then. Pushed his hat down on his head and dropped his hands over his damp crotch. "You can pay me later, *jefe*. Good night." He disappeared into the darkness.

"What was that all about, do you think, *jefe*?" The driver continued looking in the direction the worker had gone.

"I have no idea, but whatever it was scared him so much he pissed himself." Antonio dropped the spent cigarette on the ground and stamped on it. He looked out at the fields. Three tarps had been filled, and the men were hauling them over to the transport truck with Antonio's ATV. With luck, they'd be loaded and out on the road by midnight. He talked with one of the men who brought a load up to the container but was no clearer on what had happened to frighten his worker. Could have been a jaguar or a snake, the worker told him.

When the last tarp full of bud had been loaded into the container, the trap door was strapped and secured. The driver put the idling truck in gear, flashed his lights, and led the way out of the field. It was close to one o'clock in the morning. Antonio followed the transport; the highway was deserted, and the ninety kilometres would go by quickly, he thought. They continued down Highway 24 to the coast, the sea air heavy with humidity. He turned on the air conditioner, closed the windows, and cranked a CD of Gypsy Kings on the stereo.

They entered a long curve on the mountainous road. Lights from a roadside café beckoned on the other side. Antonio noticed a couple of cars in the parking lot, visible when one of them turned on its lights. As they made the final switchback and neared the café, Antonio noticed the headlights of his driver's transport flash on and off. Then, as if in response, the car in the parking lot flashed its lights. The transport didn't slow down at the café, Antonio still behind him. In the rear-view mirror he saw headlights flicker as the car pulled out of the lot and followed. Antonio flipped his cellphone open and punched in the driver's number. He answered on the second ring.

"What's happening, Pepé? Why's that car following us?"

"I have no idea, *jefe*," the driver replied. "Coincidence, probably." They continued for several minutes and then the car pulled off on a driveway leading up the mountainside.

In the distance, the lights of Corinto welcomed them like a shy young maiden hiding her beauty behind a fan. Beyond her modest illumination of the town, she was upstaged with the blazing floodlights boasting their towering presence around the harbour below. A transport idled in the lot, the driver standing with the harbourmaster who was signing papers on a clipboard. That'd be the coffee shipment, Antonio thought. As Pepé entered the loading area, Antonio parked his car in the lot outside the fence and walked down to the docks. Cranes like giant praying mantises manoeuvred their loads effortlessly, their pincers fastening onto a container, turning it, moving it closer to the freighter and depositing it on the deck without much more noise than the sound of the ship's engines.

The chubby harbourmaster finished signing and handed the clipboard to the driver. They shook hands, and the man climbed up into his idling truck. When the harbourmaster saw Antonio near the docks, he waddled over, then hugged and patted him on the back like a long-lost relative. Antonio handed him a sheaf of papers that itemized the contents of the container. He flipped the papers over and smiled. Antonio knew he had found the envelope that held his payment.

"Everything appears to be in order, Señor Vargas," the harbourmaster reported. "The boys are almost finished loading the coffee containers. Then we'll put yours on. It will leave before dawn."

"Only a couple of hours, then," Antonio said after he'd checked his watch and looked at the sky.

"No need for you to wait, Señor Vargas. You must be tired."

"Oh, I'll wait. Maybe there's a cup of coffee in the office?" The harbourmaster shrugged and trudged over to the office at the edge of the wharf. He unscrewed a thermos and poured a Styrofoam cup for Antonio and one for himself. Then he went to the window with his binoculars and looked out over the water.

"Looks calm this evening," he said to Antonio. "Good sailing." They sat down, had more coffee, and made small talk until the stevedores waved from the docks, indicating that the container had been loaded and secured. "They're ready to sail sir."

"Thanks for the coffee. I'll take the rest of it with me." Antonio stepped down from the office landing and stood at the dock, sipping his coffee and watching a tugboat pilot the freighter slowly from the docks, engines burbling; the tiny vessel leading the giant forward. Darkness was fading to the east of them, but the lights on the freighter burned bright over the dark water. Lights from another vessel flickered offshore. On and off, on and off. In minutes, the tug had shepherded the freighter out of the harbour and into open sea. Depending on weather conditions, it would take five to seven days for the freighter to arrive in San Diego harbour. Antonio tossed his empty cup in the trash can, climbed in his car, and drove south to Managua.

Traffic started to build when he got close to the capital city. He drove out the Carretera Norte to Hotel Boutique Villa Maya, close to the Augusto César Sandino Airport. While the airport honoured his great-uncle with an ultra-modern architectural structure of steel and glass, he knew that down in the centre of the sprawling congested city, a monument acknowledged his execution. Antonio preferred to remain out of the urban madness; he'd swim in the pool, watch movies, eat well, and relax. The latter was something he was going to have to learn to how to do. Slow down. He bought a Nelson DeMille mystery, and after swimming his newly enforced regime of thirty lengths each morning, he sat by the pool and read. He quickly became engrossed in the intricate terrorist plot, and when he looked up again, three hours had passed. He'd had only one cigarette and a bottle of water to drink. After lunch, he turned on the widescreen television in his room and checked the weather. The seas were calm—at least, no storms and the wind was out of the south. He went back to the pool to read.

The following day he texted the captain of the freighter to check its progress and learned that they were just south of Zihuatanejo, Mexico, and would arrive at the San Diego harbour in about two days. When he got up the next morning, Antonio booked a flight for the following day.

He pulled his car into the long-term parking area, got his suitcase from the trunk, locked it, and walked to the Departures level. When he'd checked in and cleared security, he'd only sat for a few minutes in the lounge before he heard the loading announcement. The plane was far from full. He had empty seats on either side of him, and when he'd received his coffee and muffin he settled into his book again. The next thing he knew, a flight attendant was on the intercom, advising passengers to buckle up for landing.

The San Diego Harbor was an enormous natural phenomenon that was shared by not only the U.S. Navy, but also commercial freighters, cruise ships, luxury liners, yachts, and sailboats. From the air, it looked like a gem nestled in the surrounding mountains. He spotted the berths into which the freighters were piloted and took a shot with his cellphone. With luck, his freighter would arrive tonight, to be unloaded in the morning. When he'd cleared Customs and Immigration and gathered his suitcase, he took a waiting taxi to the Hilton on Harbor Island. It was mid-afternoon. He bought another cellphone at a convenience store and called his client.

"We're on schedule, Willy," Antonio announced. He was sitting by the pool, sipping a Corona. "Our men will be in place?"

"For sure, Tony. Not a problem. Their shift begins at midnight, well in advance of the freighter docking. You've taken care of Customs. We're cool. See you in the morning for coffee in the cafeteria. We can watch it unload."

29.

VERONICA MASTERS' SKIN glowed for weeks after her trip to Costa Rica, long after her tan had faded. Her time with Simon remained firmly etched in her memory. She recounted incidents, gestures, and conversations that featured so largely in her mind that she had to fight with herself not to pick up the phone.

He seemed to have enjoyed her company, too, she thought. It was easy being with him or being alone on the beach. They had moved harmoniously, she thought. It was amusing that Don Verde could pronounce her name perfectly; more so, when she realized that it would had to have been repeated many times for the bird to learn to say it. She was grateful for whatever sense she and Simon had had that night when they almost, but didn't, tumble into bed. It would have been delicious, no doubt, but if it hadn't been, if their chemistry hadn't clicked, their little romp in the hay might well have tainted their working relationship.

One of the nights they'd had a bonfire on the beach, Simon had asked her if she thought she could live in such a quasi-remote place, and she'd found it difficult to answer. Since then, she daydreamed about living at the beach, of starting a new routine, snorkelling or bodysurfing or jogging. At least jogging on the sand would be more forgiving than pounding on pavement, which she'd given up after suffering from shin splints while jogging in Central Park. But she wasn't able to answer the question of what she would do for income. Granted, she wouldn't need as much. She could be more casual, own fewer clothes. Sandals would cut down on shoe leather. Expenses would be minimal. But what would she do for money? Sell the gallery in Soho? Keep the gallery and commute once a month? That would be costly. Open a gallery in one of the resorts somewhere near Simon? She didn't know the urban areas in Costa Rica, only Liberia, coming from the airport. Anyway, she was projecting. She had a gallery to run and Simon's exhibition in the future—the far-too-distant future.

30.

"THAT'S A SHITLOAD of money," Antonio whispered, unnecessarily, because they were secure in their apartment with the doors locked. They were counting the spoils from the bulk sale on their pot harvest, dividing it equally.

Antonio had paid everyone: the field workers, driver, harbourmaster at the port in Corinto, and the Customs official in San Diego. When it came right down to it, greed figured centre stage in every walk of life. For ten thousand dollars, the harbourmaster in Corinto had turned a blind eye when their container was loaded. When it reached San Diego, Antonio had been there to see the deal through. He'd paid the Customs official to avert his eyes. He was a buddy who'd made easy money before and was always hungry for more. Antonio's buyer was there with the tractor-trailer and they both sipped espresso while they watched the container being off-loaded from the freighter and into the truck. Within an hour, Antonio had been in a jet to Managua and was back in Granada by nightfall. He and Marco estimated that after those hefty expenses, they had each made two million dollars.

Stacks of twenties, fifties, and one-hundred-dollar bills covered the bed. Antonio was caressing it like the proud, loving father of a newborn baby. "Glad I opened those bank accounts; now's the time to start renting safety deposit boxes. What are you going to do with yours, Marco?"

Marco was leaning against the frame of the doorway to the

balcony, looking out in the direction of Laguna de Apoyo. "I think it's time to change my karma," he mused, still looking in the distance.

"How do you propose to do that?" Antonio asked. He was now lying among the stacks of currency.

"By making amends with some of the women in the world."

"Whatever you say, Marco. Sounds pretty far-out to me."

"We'll see."

31.

IT WASN'T AS EASY as you think, Antonio. You live in a dream world. The harvest went well, but you weren't aware that one of your workers was attempting to steal you blind—until he wet his pants in fear when I appeared before him in the fields. You arrived to oversee the transport of the container, but once again, temptation and greed infected your well-paid driver. How difficult would it be to open the container and off-load some of the contents to one of his compadres? One phone call when he left the fields and they would rendezvous in a truck stop along the highway. No problem. Except when he called his buddy, I appeared beside him in the cab and he quickly dropped the phone. I don't know whether he actually wet his pants or not.

And your so-called buddy, the harbourmaster? What a joke! You should know better, Tonio. As soon as the container was loaded and you paid him off, and after you'd left, he called the Coast Guard, gave them the coordinates they'd be travelling so that they could intercept. They planned to share the spoils and sell it, but they missed the interception because their vessel's gas line clogged.You knew that the freighter continued on to San Diego without incident and was piloted into Customs. You knew the official—you had supposedly "worked" with him before—but what you didn't know was that he had also been infected with the greed germ. When the shipment of coffee was off-loaded and he'd signed off on it, he motioned for his crane operator,who wasn't yet on duty—not yours—to haul the container to a scow that was waiting at the edge of the wharf. Except that when the driver went to climb up into the crane, he caught his boot on the frame of the cabin and tripped, toppling onto the wharf. He was winded and couldn't get up right away. He reached for the hand one of his buddies offered, but as he yanked him up, he too, lost his footing and together they splashed into the water. I appeared before the Customs official and advised him to deliver on his part of the deal with you, Antonio. He appeared shaken. He smelled, Antonio. I think he'd soiled himself. And you got your "shitload of money."

32.

WHEN MARCO WALKED into her shop, Sylvia was measuring a length of material, pins in her mouth. "Happy Valentine's Day, Sylvia." He handed her a bouquet of long-stemmed, red roses.

She quickly took the pins out of her mouth and received the flowers with a wide smile on her face. "Oh, thank you, Marco. No one has ever given me roses." She held them against her nose and breathed deeply. "They're gorgeous. Such a sweet fragrance."

"You deserve roses every day. Not just today," he said. "I don't want to keep you from your work. I just wanted to wish you a good day and to invite you to dinner this evening. What do you say?"

"Wonderful, Marco. I'd love to."

"I'll come by about six o'clock and we can walk up to the *mirador*." He walked back to the door. "Oh, yes, and I lit a candle for you this morning."

At dinner that night, the restaurant pulsed with flickering candles. Ropes of scarlet hearts festooned the balcony railings, and the atmosphere was celestial. They had boarded a ship of dreams that sailed above the lake. Marco reached for Sylvia's hands, lifted one to his lips and kissed it. "Would you be free for a little while tomorrow morning?" he asked. "I'd like to show you a place I'm thinking of buying. I'd like your opinion." She nodded and smiled. She was itching with curiosity but didn't push it. They enjoyed their meal, the wine, and their time together.

He picked her up at nine o'clock the following morning, and they drove down the mountain to Laguna de Apoyo. "I really believe this is a healing place," Marco told her.

"I felt that way too when I first arrived. Then I learned it's protected from development, so perhaps, in gratitude, the lake protects the people who care for it."

As they drove further down the mountain, the air grew noticeably warmer. Over the lake, little wisps of remaining fog drifted like gossamer. Marco pulled up on a circular driveway made of volcanic rock.

"*Dios mio*!" Sylvia exclaimed. She put her hands to her mouth. "It's a palace, Marco, enormous."

The grounds were well-kept. Hedges of bougainvillea spilled over the stone walls on the edges of the expansive lakeside property. Flaming lantanas, fragrant lilies, and roses had been planted in borders along the front of the house. Marco knocked on the iron-studded wooden door, and almost immediately, it was opened by Yolanda, the housekeeper. She'd known they were coming and welcomed them, told them to feel free to walk about. It was or would soon be their house, she added. Sylvia blushed and looked up at Marco who said nothing but smiled.

A wide, central staircase graciously divided the house. To their left was a large dining room and a huge commercial-strength kitchen with a walk-in refrigerated room, an eight-burner gas range with a copper hood, a butcher block in the centre, and miles of counter space for food preparation. Over the butcher block, dangling from a pan rack, were iron frying pans and copper saucepans.

"Look at this kitchen. You could start a restaurant." Sylvia gazed around as if she'd landed on another planet.

"You can do anything you want here, Sylvia. No rent and no strings attached." They entered the living room where the centre wall was a fireplace made out of the ubiquitous dark volcanic rock. A large half-circle of down-filled furniture faced the fireplace; between chesterfield and fireplace a bevelled glass table sparkled in the morning light. Floor-to-ceiling casement windows looked onto the placid lake. They climbed the wide wooden staircase; railings and a gallery gave onto the bedrooms, each with its own bathroom.

"I can't believe the size of this place, Marco." Sylvia's eyes were wide, unblinking.

"And it comes furnished," Marco added. "You can keep Yolanda, too, if you want. She's pleasant and knows the ropes here. I can talk to her if you want."

"I couldn't afford to pay her, Marco."

"Don't worry about that. I'll take care of it."

"It will cost you a fortune. How can you have so much money? Did you rob a bank? Did you get an inheritance?"

"Something like that." Marco let the ambiguity float between them. "Let me just say that a very large investment paid off and the cost of this place is paid for by the interest alone."

Sylvia's eyes grew even wider, but she didn't comment or respond. He would have to level with her at some point, he thought. But now wasn't the time. She might refuse to live in the house or operate a shelter for battered women, if she knew it was paid for with laundered money.

They walked down to the beach. Silence and tranquility, Sylvia thought. "This place would be perfect for a shelter. I feel so calm here."

"You should probably think about hiring a watchman in case angry husbands come looking for their women."

"More money," she said.

"Don't worry about it. Write down what you need, what it will cost, and I can deposit it in your account each month."

They walked out to the end of the dock where a rowboat was tied. The paddles were in the bottom of the craft. "Have we got time for a paddle?" Marco asked.

"We can make time. I can't imagine that Lidia is run off her feet." Sylvia took Marco's hand and climbed into the boat. When she was seated, he untied the rope and jumped in. He fastened the oars into their locks and began to row. The crater lake was crystal clear. He rowed halfway across. Above them was the *mirador* at Catarina. Back on the shore was the hacienda: stately and rustically elegant.

Marco would buy the house; it would be in his name, but Sylvia could live there rent-free as could other women. He was determined to be philanthropic with his ill-gotten gains.

33.

WHEN SYLVIA RETURNED to her shop, Lidia was bent over the cutting table, pinning a pattern onto powder blue silk. "How did it go?" Lidia asked as she looked up from her work.

"Incredible, Lidia. The place is enormous. There are six bedrooms, all with ensuite baths, some with balconies. The kitchen is commercially outfitted—it even has a walk-in refrigerator. We rowed out on the lake, and when I looked back, it was like a dream. The gardens are beautiful, the grounds are spacious, and a gardener and housekeeper come with the place if I wish." She took up a scrap of the silk from the table and drew it back and forth between her fingers.

"We'll have to take in more sewing," Lidia said, her eyes pensive. "Maybe I'll make some flyers and take them down to San Juan de Oriente and a few other places nearby."

"That's just it. We don't even have to work if we don't want to," Sylvia said, smiling broadly.

Lidia looked at her and laughed.

"Seriously," Sylvia continued. "Marco says he will take care of their salaries, and if we want to take in any other women who need shelter, he will hire a watchman, too. The house will be in his name, but you and I and anyone else can live there free. *Dios mio,* we could open a restaurant with that kitchen!"

"Where do you think he got all that money?" Lidia was back to her work, cutting the pinned material.

"I didn't press him for more information, but he said he did very well on some investments and that this purchase is covered by the interest alone."

"That could mean anything." Lidia didn't look up.

"But he's such a nice man. See that bowl of dried red rose petals over there? You remember that he gave me a dozen roses for Valentine's Day. He lights candles and prays for me. I can't imagine that he's a criminal."

"Well, think what you will about him. But neither of us thought that our husbands—the men we loved and married—would beat us either."

34.

ANTONIO BOUGHT A LAPTOP and extended their cable contract with Claro Americas to include internet access. He spent his days on the terrace in the shade of the canvas, surfing the internet for real estate, particularly islands on Lake Nicaragua. There were a few that were being sold privately. One day, he hired a launch and toured the lake, looking at the private listings, making notes, sizing each place up in terms of liveability. He found one that had a large main house, a completely outfitted and separate cabin, a party gazebo with a sunken Jacuzzi in the centre of it—as well as a swimming pool. When Nick's buddy returned and wanted his house back, Nick could live in the cottage, and the house would be large enough for Marco and himself.

As the deal on the property was being drawn up and the deed searched, he bought a fibreglass boat and motor, and leased a slip near the foot of Calle La Calzada. He started to make preparations to move when the deal closed in May.

"You should see it, Marco," he yelled in Marco's direction. Antonio was at the fridge getting a beer. "Want one?" He grabbed two bottles, opened them, and carried them out to the terrace where Marco was sitting with his feet up on one of the chairs. They'd both gotten into buying real estate. Antonio was impressed with the hacienda Marco had purchased and thought it was a good move. "When you've got time, we'll take a zip around and look at the place I'm thinking about."

The owners of the island property lived and worked in Managua; the island had been their holiday retreat. The next day, Antonio and Marco motored over, tied up at the double-sided slip and climbed the steps to the main house. They peeked in through the curtainless windows. The rooms were bright and spacious; the ceramic tile floors dazzled, and sunlight filtered through the leaves of an enormous tree whose buttressed roots spanned several metres. Yellow pompoms covered the tips of every branch as did the mauling bees that pollinated them. The men looked up, diminutive beneath its magnificence.

"A Kapok tree," Antonio said. His hand was on its warty bark.

"We call them Ceiba in Costa Rica." Marco looked up into the branches. "Look," he whispered. "A quetzal. Maybe they nest here." He patted the bark thoughtfully. "Man, they say this mother can grow to be over sixty metres tall. Must be halfway there already and I won't live long enough to see it mature."

"So what do you think, Marco?"

"Looks like a great place, Antonio. Not as refreshing as the apartment at Catarina, though."

"I would have bought that place if it was for sale, but this is definitely more private; it's what, midday, and there's a breeze. Not bad." He looked about him, then continued. "Anyway, I have a suite at the hacienda at Laguna de Apoyo and can stay there whenever I want. This should work out nicely."

Before they went back to the mainland, they sat for a few minutes watching the birds, iguanas, and lizards that darted through the foliage.

35.

SYLVIA GAVE NOTICE to her landlord and advised her customers that she would be moving her business down to the lake. Six weeks later, she and Lidia packed the contents of the house and shop, and Marco hired a truck and driver. He carefully loaded all of their potted plants into the back of his SUV and drove Sylvia and Lidia down to the house.

"I feel like a princess in a castle," Sylvia said. "I've never had so much space in my life." Nor had Lidia, who stood in the middle of the living room, turning and turning like a pirouetting ballerina with her arms extended. Marco left them in their newfound bliss, pleased that he had been able to offer it.

"Imagine being rewarded for being beaten, scorned, and abused." They had prepared a stir-fry with rice and salad, and when they finished eating, they moved from the dining room to the veranda where they were sharing a bottle of wine that was Marco's housewarming gift.

"Perhaps this is our next life, and the good energy we put into the previous one determined how our lives would be in this one," Lidia suggested. "Like karma. And that old expression, 'what goes around, comes around.' If only my husband had understood that before he laid a hand on me."

Word spread that there was a safe haven, a shelter for abused women, and the hacienda shone like a beacon for shipwrecked sailors. Two women appeared, three days apart, one with blackened eyes and a cut by her lip that had required seven stitches.

The other woman had a broken arm and bruises. Both were in shock but visibly grateful for the respite. In the meantime, Sylvia and Lidia continued to repair, alter, and create clothes for women.

True to his word, Marco found a trustworthy man whom he hired to guard the house at night. Yolanda, the housekeeper and José, the gardener, remained on staff and watched the property during the day. Hiring a night watchman had been a wise decision, because one week after the two new women had arrived, one of their drunken husbands had staggered onto the property, cursing and calling his wife's name. The police were called, and he was taken away and slapped with a restraining order.

The two women who had joined them in the house also had some experience sewing and took on projects they were confident they could handle. Broken bones mended, stitches were removed, bruises faded, and the good meals Yolanda cooked put meat on their bony frames. After evening meals, they all sat around the firepit near the shore and shared stories: funny, sad, mysterious, and miraculous. They made each other laugh and cry, and most of all, heal.

Marco drove Sylvia and the other women to mass one Sunday morning. They'd arrived early and all sat in the same pew. The sermon was based on the theme of forgiveness: To forgive those who had hurt you; to ask forgiveness from those to whom you had been unkind; and to forgive yourself. Marco noticed that a couple of the women were weeping, probably remembering their husbands.

When Marco prayed, he asked Isabella to forgive him. He prayed, asking for forgiveness from his unborn child, for the harm he had caused them. Hard as he tried, he couldn't forgive himself, but perhaps God could.

36.

A FULL MOON SLASHED silver blades across the still water. I'd finished washing up the day's dishes and strolled down to the beach to watch the play of light on the rippling waves. Don Verde flitted back and forth, sometimes coming to rest on my shoulder. About a mile out, a freighter appeared to be at anchor, something I'd never seen. I stood at the shoreline and tried to see if it moved. It didn't. Don Verde landed on my shoulder and acted agitated, kneading his claws into my flesh. Into my ear he said, clear as a bell, "*Viaje muy lejos*"—a long trip. He flew a short distance over the water and returned to my shoulder.

I continued to watch the freighter. It wasn't moving. Then, a bright lemon-yellow dinghy or zodiac was lowered over the side. Don Verde paraded up and down my shoulder saying, "*Viaje muy lejos; mucho dinero.*"

The dinghy appeared to be coming towards me and as it neared, Don Verde became even more vocal. The driver cut the motor and drifted closer to shore. Don Verde flew into a nearby tree.

"*Buenas noches*," said the man from the dinghy. I repeated the greeting. Then he started in rapid-fire Spanish and lost me. He was looking for someone and motioned to the house. I understood that he had tried to telephone, but there was no answer. I tried to explain in my feeble Spanish that I was the new owner, that there had been a murder at the house. He understood me, I know, for his chiselled facial features took on new angles. He bowed and tried unsuccessfully to hurry through the water. He climbed into the dinghy and dropped the motor. On his second pull, it started, and he fled. Or at least that's what it looked like to me.

37.

WHILE HE WAITED to move to his island home, Antonio ran into Hector Cortez, an old acquaintance, a pilot he'd hired a few times. They were having lunch on the patio outside the Café de los Sueños. Hector was telling him about a plane that was for sale.

"It's a beauty. It has pontoons, but it's also equipped with a wheel undercarriage on the floats so it can touch down on both water and land. Hell, I could be in the air eighty percent of the time, hauling people and cargo with a plane like that," he lamented.

"Maybe I could help you out, Hector, and keep you busy the other twenty percent of the time, too." Antonio rubbed his jaw and thought while Hector rhymed off a confusing list of specs on the craft, fuelling the notion.

"I've flown the baby," Hector said. "Hired on to pilot executives to Managua. She moves like a dream. Very economical." He looked at Antonio and didn't know if he'd been listening or not.

"I would buy the plane and lease it out to you but also have access to both you and the craft should I need to move something or go somewhere. I told you I was moving to the island, and I think there's room to tie it up over there." They both grew animated thinking about the prospect.

Hector made a call to the owner while Antonio paid the bill. Then, together, they drove down to the harbour where the plane was moored. The owner pulled up shortly after them. The tank was full; he handed Hector the keys. Antonio climbed in, and the owner untied the ropes before jumping on board. The engine was loud, and they were unable to speak until after Hector had taxied beyond the boats into open water, nosed into the air, and levelled out. He looked across at Antonio and grinned. "Where to, sir?"

Antonio directed them to the archipelago of islands where his house was situated. They circled the island, high above the crown of the giant golden Ceiba tree from which they flushed the resident quetzal, its streamer-like green tail feathers drifting in the breeze, its red breast a ball of fire blazing in the sunlight as it flew ahead of them and landed on another islet, waiting. Hector slowed the plane and splashed into the water near the docks. The double-sided slip would be perfect to secure the plane when Antonio needed it; Hector would have to find a slip on the mainland. Antonio nodded that he was satisfied, and they flew back to Granada.

Later in the day, Hector and Antonio met with the owner to give him the cash. They transferred the ownership with a notary and took possession. They returned to the Café de los Sueños and had a beer in celebration of their new acquisition. They worked out a lease agreement and talked about how Hector could get word out that he was in business. Antonio had just laundered another few thousand dollars and would make money in return.

38.

SINCE HE WOULD be living on an island made of volcanic rock with little or no soil, there was no point in trying to move all his plants over there from Catarina, so Marco hired a large cube van and carefully transferred them to the hacienda on Laguna de Apoyo where he and the gardener transplanted them. And since the house Antonio and Marco were moving into came furnished, they sold pieces they'd bought for the apartment and took only lamps, kitchen utensils, and their clothes.

In the midst of it all, Nick Bacon had called and announced that he needed to find a place, since his friend, the owner of the house he was living in, was back in town. Antonio told him about the cottage, and sight unseen, it was a done deal. Nick would move over a month after Antonio and Marco had settled.

They packed their belongings in both cars and drove to the dock where the guide boats moored, one of which Antonio had hired for a couple of hours. They loaded their things on the launch, then drove to a secured parking lot on the mainland and took a taxi back to the boat. They were at the dock on the islet in less than a half-hour, unloaded, and soon after, Antonio was barbecuing chicken for Marco and the driver.

39.

IN EARLY OCTOBER, I packed a bag and boxed up my paintings for New York. I'd asked Maria if she could come by occasionally to dust, water the plants, and generally keep an eye on the place. Don Verde would miss me; he might even take off without any company. We had become good friends during the past few months, and I would miss him if he wasn't here when I got back, so I phoned Maria again and asked if she would consider staying in the house, and that I would pay her for her time. She accepted. She explained that she was alone at home most of the time, anyway, since her children were grown up and living all over the country, and her husband drove transport trucks throughout Central America. I was only in Maria's home once, and I remembered it as being airless and tiny and close to other houses. She would enjoy the breeze at my hacienda on the beach—and get paid for the effort.

It was the first time I'd been in the air since I had moved to Costa Rica. At this time of year, as we flew over the U.S., the landscape below me was ablaze; maples and sumac splashed red amid bright yellow poplar and beech. Veronica had offered to collect me at the airport, but I had declined, saying it was too expensive and counterproductive. I told her I would go directly to my friend's loft; he was in Paris and was relieved that I'd be staying there. I unpacked, showered, and took a taxi to the gallery.

When I got there, I quickly learned that Veronica had taken

advantage of my early arrival and had set up an interview with a journalist and photographer from a local art publication. Another magazine had already laid out an article with some of the high-resolution digital images Veronica had provided. They were hoping to make their deadline. All they needed was to take a photo of me and write a suitable cutline. The gallery had spent a lot of money on advertising and invitations; we could only hope for the best.

Veronica lived only about two blocks from where I was staying, so each day after the gallery closed, we met for a drink at my loft or hers, reflected on the day's framing, the items I'd ticked off my to-do list, and decided what to do for dinner. We each cooked a couple of nights a week, making a shopping expedition together to buy the fresh Atlantic salmon at a fishmonger Veronica knew, or Angus rib-eye steaks from her favourite butcher. The balance of the time, we went out to restaurants. As we walked from the gallery to my place, I saw our reflection in the plate glass window of a store. My freshly cut, usually blond hair, was fading to white, but still held its own admirably. I was a couple of inches taller than Veronica; the top of her curly red head reached my cheekbone. I looked at us objectively and saw a handsome couple.

One morning, I decided to do some shopping. I'd been a year out of fashion and I needed some new duds for the opening, so I went to Bloomingdale's. And who did I happen to meet on the escalator? Ingrid. Her face flushed visibly, hopefully still embarrassed by what she had done. I felt nothing. I smiled when she complimented my tan. When we stepped off the escalator, she told me how good I looked. I thanked her and continued on to the men's shoe department. She followed me.

"It didn't work out," she blurted, her voice quavering like she was going to cry. "I broke up with him. I haven't been seeing anyone."

"And you want me to take up the slack, I suppose." I didn't look at her and continued fingering the soft leather of an Italian loafer. “I’ve moved on, Ingrid. I’m just visiting.”

“Yes. I read about your upcoming show at the Lasting Image Gallery,” she said. “I’d like to see your new work.”

“It’s open to the public. You’re more than welcome to come,” I said. Before I could add anything, a sales associate came up to me, so I didn’t get the opportunity to tell her that this time she wouldn’t have a snowball’s chance in hell of bedding this gallery owner.

40.

ONE OF THE WOMEN staying at the hacienda carried a sketch pad with her everywhere and drew whatever came into her mind. Sometimes images of nightmarish ghouls and dark creatures leapt off the page. As she spent more time in the tranquil supportive environment at the hacienda, she started sketching aspects of the landscape, such as flowers, iguanas, and birds. The women commented that the new images indicated she was functioning in the present, that she was able to see what was around her, and that the initial sketches had been exorcisms from her soul. After a few weeks, she started sketching dresses and outfits that would have impressed *Vogue* magazine editors. She showed them to Sylvia and smiled when Sylvia pinned them to the wall of their workshop area and attempted to draw, then cut patterns. They purchased three mannequins on which they displayed the new dresses. Some of the women who came to drop off clothes to be repaired or collect alterations saw them and immediately placed orders. Sylvia kept a file of their clients' dimensions, and if the women hadn't been dieting or gained weight, they were able to finish the work quickly and efficiently without remeasuring or scheduling fitting sessions.

The kitchen was brought up to working condition. Yolanda drew up a small menu of hot and iced coffees and teas, fruit drinks, sandwiches, and cakes, which she served on the terrace where soft instrumental music drifted on the air, the atmosphere much like a café at a resort. Sylvia and Lidia's clients appeared to enjoy themselves as they relaxed and stayed much longer than they ever had at the little shop in Catarina.

Sylvia saw Marco several times a week. They went out for lunch or Yolanda made dinner for them. Sometimes, they all ate together in the dining room with the other women; occasionally, they'd eat alone by candlelight on the terrace.

"I've started rowing, Marco," Sylvia told him one night. "Can I take you out for a paddle under the moonlight?" There was laughter in her voice.

"Only if you let me row back."

Yolanda arrived just then to take their plates and asked if they wanted coffee.

"Maybe later, Yolanda," said Sylvia. "We're going out on the lake now. Go home when you want. I can make the coffee if we want any when we come back."

Smiling their goodbyes to Yolanda, they turned and walked down to the dock.

Sylvia's sculling was strong and efficient. They were halfway across the lake in no time. They sat in the middle of the lake beneath the fullness of an ivory-coloured moon and drifted whichever way the wind took them. They were both leaning against either side of the boat, their legs extended across the seats. "I don't think I've ever been happier, Marco," Sylvia said as the boat rocked gently.

"That makes me happy, Sylvia. I'm glad that your business has grown since you've come here. And that the women are happy here."

"Oh, yes. I think we are learning about ourselves through sharing our experiences. Some buried so deep and for so long that the emotional release—for all of us—is profound. We make each other laugh and cry. Both necessary emotions." She leaned forward so she could see his face. "Why are you being so kind to me? To us? What have we done to deserve such generous gifts?"

"I think it's called karmic house cleaning."

She giggled.

"No, seriously," Marco insisted. He swung his legs around, sat up straight in his seat, and cleared his throat. "As I told you before, a rather large investment gained substantially in value, and how you are able to live here is from the interest on that investment. That's the truth." Marco paused and searched his pockets for a cigarette, then remembered he'd quit. He took a deep breath, and when he exhaled, he continued. "What I omitted was that we were selling drugs and because we can't claim to have earned such large amounts of money, we are laundering it through real estate. And you are the beneficiaries."

"What if the police arrive one day and confiscate the house?" Sylvia had straightened in her seat and folded her arms across her chest.

"That's not going to happen, Sylvia. The shipment made it safely out of the country two months ago. We got paid handsomely and paid those working for us. We aren't going to do it again. It was a one-time deal. There is no investigation, and there *will be* no investigation. The product is on the market and has probably gone through several levels of distribution and ownership since we sold it. So, this house is free and clear of any investigation. You have nothing to worry about."

Sylvia remained silent with her arms wrapped around her like she was chilled. She squirmed a bit on the seat, wrestling with something unseen.

"Nothing to worry about. Except that my landlord is a criminal who lights candles and says prayers for me and others." She laughed derisively. "Are we praying to the same God or is there a crime god?" She laughed even harder. "I can't believe you are telling me this. What else are you going to tell me?" She set the paddles in the water.

"Remember, you were going to let me row back." Without speaking, they gingerly changed places and Marco rowed to shore. They tied the boat to the dock and started back to the house. Sylvia marched ahead, but Marco caught up with her and grabbed her hand. She didn't fight him. When they were halfway across the garden, near the lipstick palms, he stopped, causing her to stop. His back was to the house; he spoke quietly.

"I admit I've made a lot of money selling drugs. It is an illegal activity, granted, but many other activities are illegal and the powers that be turn blind eyes. Many of those powerful officials are up to their necks in this activity themselves and are getting paid to turn their heads. There is an incredibly large market—buying and using are also illegal. So, we are all felons in this game. When Antonio and I met, we had a goal we wanted to reach, and we've made it. Period. Game over. Early retirement. We've been very careful. Our methods have been modest, creative, unique, and never duplicated. It was an exciting career, we made a lot of money, but it's over. I hope you believe me."

Her eyes were fixed on his, and he shuddered. Then her lips started to curl, blossoming to a smile, lighting the shadows that had been lurking around them. He drew her near, kissed her hand, and then raised his face close to hers. "May I kiss you?" he whispered. Her smile widened, and she licked her lips. "Yes," she whispered back.

He put his arm around her and kissed her tenderly. Briefly. When neither of them moved, he kissed her again and wrapped his arms around her; he felt her arms on his shoulders, her fingers combing through his wavy black hair. They leaned against each other in an intimate silence.

"I think I'm falling in love with you, Sylvia."

41.

MARCO FELT LIKE he was seeing less of Antonio since they had moved to the island. He knew he'd bought a laptop but hadn't realized that Antonio would be spending so much time on it. One morning after he'd poured a coffee, Marco looked over Antonio's shoulder and saw that he was studying a map of Granada.

"What are you up to, Tonio?"

"Doing a little research," Antonio replied, not looking up from the screen. "I think I've found the tunnel that runs from William Walker's house."

"So, what's the big deal?" Marco asked, shrugging.

Antonio looked up from the computer and swivelled in his chair to face Marco. "I guess I haven't been keeping you in the loop, bro. We've been into our own things. You with your women's shelter and all. Anyway, I have been looking at the foundation of the area around Granada. Nick Bacon, the ex-Marine I told you I met a few months ago—the guy who's going to move into the cottage—well, he and I have been working on something. I told you he was into plastic explosives in the Middle East. He showed me one of the programs he'd written for the Marines. Pretty cool shit."

"What's this all leading up to, Antonio?" Marco was sprawled on a sofa, sipping his coffee. He noticed that Antonio had taken on a new persona; he was using new words and phrases that must have come from Nick Bacon.

"He's feeding a map with all the information I can find in the next few months, and when we find the end of the tunnel, we'll see which bank it is closest to. I bet it's the one furthest north on Calle Atravesada. When we know that, we'll work our way towards it, planting explosives that we'll detonate, little by little. It can all be done with a cellphone, Marco! Little earth-moving blasts at first. And before Christmas, we'll be there. When we get to the area where the safety deposit boxes are located, we do the big blast and open it up. We go in, grab the goods, and split."

Marco jolted upright, splashing coffee on his bare thighs. He stood and wiped his legs with a napkin. "Are you out of your mind? I thought you said we'd retire after that last shipment. That we'd be set for life."

"We are, man. We are. I just love the idea of doing this during all the fireworks of La Purísima. Not a soul will hear us. Remember the noise and how we jumped at every blast? How sometimes we couldn't hear each other speak? It's the perfect time for a crime. I love the idea."

"Why don't you just leave it at that, an idea? Mental calisthenics. You're many things, Antonio. You're smart, you're creative, and you're a great salesman, but what you're *not* is a thief." Marco got up and went to the kitchen to get more coffee. Then he continued outside to sit by the pool.

Antonio followed him. "I thought you knew the plan, Marco."

"You alluded to a fantastic idea during La Purísima—during all of December. We moved to Catarina to get away from the noise, remember? But that's all I thought it was: a fantastic idea. I want nothing to do with it." Marco lay back and shut his eyes then sat up again. "And I may be many things, but I'm not a thief, either."

"Have it your way, bro." Antonio went back inside.

Marco lay in the shade and thought about Antonio's preposterous plan. For some reason, he didn't feel guilty about selling large quantities of marijuana or small quantities of cocaine, for that matter. He didn't feel like a criminal. But robbing a bank? When they already had millions of dollars invested in property? Robbing a bank would be a death wish. He'd just told Sylvia that he had retired from the smuggling business. She'd run so fast if she learned that he and his partner were going to rob a bank. He wanted her trust more than anything. He felt closer to her now than ever and didn't want to lose her.

42.

MY EXHIBITION WAS A SELLOUT, beyond my wildest expectations. Veronica and her staff had handled the publicity well. The ads had been effective, and I received good coverage. My ex was there for the opening, but by then it was obvious that Veronica and I were more than business associates. Any inhibitions we had had in Costa Rica—or perhaps the control we had practised—had been tossed out the window during my first night in the city.

We'd gone out to a neighbourhood trattoria for some clam pasta and red wine, both of us animated and energized, probably about the exhibition, but more likely from the sparks that might have been visible between us. We somehow managed to finish dinner, and I paid the bill. Then we walked arm in arm, breathing in the crisp fall air, to her place.

Her loft was spacious, open, and beautiful, with two walls of exposed red brick and a wall of windows, now with curtains drawn. A gas fireplace started with the flick of a switch and provided both warmth and atmosphere. I browsed her music collection while she made coffee. Her taste was eclectic: jazz, pop, folk artists, some Gaelic CDs, even a couple of didgeridoo recordings. I selected Stan Getz' *Finest Hour* compilation, one I hadn't heard in a long time.

Veronica walked in from the kitchen just as the sultry, sensual riffs of "It Never Entered My Mind" oozed from the speakers. She set the tray of coffee on the table and held out her arms to me. "May I have this dance?" she asked.

The highly lacquered pine plank floors were perfect for dancing. We moved well together, melded as one, floating in space. The piece ended, and we lingered on the dance floor, hanging on to each other for a moment before sitting on the couch to drink our coffee. She'd doctored them both with Baileys, something else I hadn't had in a long time.

The goose down sofa enveloped us as we both dreamily gazed into the fire. She was tucked in under my arm, head on my chest. Awkward to kiss that way, and she finally realized that, too. She sat up, put her arms around me, and initiated what would be a kiss of marathon proportions. We only stopped for air and to change position so that we were lying together. There may have been a guest room, but I didn't sleep there—ever. I stood and carried her into her bedroom where we continued our dance, undressing, exploring, and caressing each other. We made love and it was exquisite, satisfying, and ultimately exhausting. We saw the first hint of dawn and finally surrendered to sleep.

Veronica was leaning on her elbow, looking at me, when I opened my eyes. "Hi you," I said. My voice was octaves deeper than I remembered it. I smiled.

"How did you sleep?" she asked.

"Well. Very well." I traced her lips with my finger.

"And as we're still lying together, I gather there is no remorse? No guilt?"

"A rhetorical question, my dear." I threw my arms around her and rolled her on top of me. "I think the answer is fairly obvious." And that made her late for work.

43.

BY THE TIME SYLVIA said good night to Marco, all the women had retired to their rooms. She lit a candle and some incense and sat on the sofa with the lights off, attempting to understand what had just happened. She was living in a house that had been purchased with laundered drug money. Marco claimed that he was out of the business and that he was falling in love with her. Like that game in which you tell three things about yourself and only one is true, she wondered which, if *any*, was.

She couldn't understand how he could be so religious and still be involved in criminal activity. But as he had said, even government officials and members of the police force were not immune to this kind of business. She still remembered a photograph in a newspaper she'd seen as a teenager of a government official helping to load bags full of illegal drugs onto a plane. Yes, it was a lucrative business, but nevertheless illegal. She knew there were a lot of people who took drugs; some smoked marijuana, others snorted cocaine. Many were strung out on pills, which they purchased illegally or coerced their doctors to prescribe more than they should, and that was illegal, too. But did this make what he had done okay? Perhaps he was telling the truth. She told herself that it was in all in the past, and that he was different now. She wanted it to be true. She liked him, and like him, she thought she might be falling in love. But it was so confusing.

44.

MARCO HAD TO DEPEND on water taxis when Antonio was in town with the boat. He didn't know if living on an island was going to work. It was a beautiful place, granted. But the idea of being isolated, dependent on a fifteen-minute boat ride to town took the spontaneity out of doing anything. He wasn't going to buy a boat because he didn't think this life was for him. Perhaps on a larger, populated island like San Andrés in Colombia, he could handle it. But right now, his focus was on Laguna de Apoyo and Sylvia.

She was doing tremendously well. Not only was she helping other women, but they were producing a beautiful line of clothing. He'd seen the most recent dresses, first on the mannequins, and then modelled by one of Sylvia's customers. She was a gorgeous woman, and when she'd walked through the café, other customers applauded. Marco and Sylvia had been sitting at a table while one of the women assisted another customer with her dress. When she came onto the terrace to model the dress, she was beaming, then turned to Sylvia and suggested she produce a fashion show.

Sylvia turned to look at Marco, her soft brown eyes peering over her coffee mug. "What do you think?" she asked.

"The place could certainly accommodate a lot of people. It's a wonderful setting. We'd have to rent some tables and chairs, but it's definitely doable." Marco looked at the staircase alongside the patio. "The models could dress upstairs and make their entrance from the staircase. With spotlights, it would be fabulous."

Marco leaned in close, and put his hand over Sylvia's. "I have a surprise for you," he said.

He explained he'd met an old friend the previous day when he was walking through the market in Granada. Trina Marquez was a massage therapist he'd met when she was still in school. She had a car, a portable massage table, and made house calls. He asked her if she would drive up to Laguna de Apoyo and set up her table for five appointments throughout the course of a day. Of course, she'd said. Marco grinned at Sylvia. "So, she is going to drive up and give all five of you massages, my treat."

"There are only four of us here," Sylvia said, grinning back at him.

"What about Yolanda? She would probably love a massage."

Marco handed his cellphone over to Sylvia, and asked her to call Trina so they could pick a mutually convenient day.

The women at the hacienda loved Trina. One of Sylvia's customers, who had observed her work at the first appointment, booked a massage for the following day. Soon, Sylvia had set up a spare bedroom for Trina and her table, and it wasn't long before she was booked for two full days a week.

A fashion show was in the works. The woman who had done the sketches for the dresses created a few sample posters and they chose one. Their customers told their friends, and word of mouth spread like a delicious rumour. A newspaper editor even called and sent a reporter to take photographs before the show—some free publicity for them. If the women were concerned about their abusive husbands coming, they said nothing. Their newfound income and the comfort of their protective shelter seemed to give them confidence.

45.

I LEFT MANHATTAN with a healthy bank account, a full wallet, and new clothes that I probably wouldn't wear again for a while. But sadly, I also left without Veronica. We had spent the most part of three weeks together, working, playing, loving, and sharing our lives. During my time there in the city where I had spent most of my adult life, I saw landmarks that appeared new to me, as though I was a tourist and it was my inaugural visit to the Big Apple.

It was mid-November. This Christmas and New Year's, Veronica would be here with me in Costa Rica. We had done a lot of daydreaming, vocalizing "what if" propositions and trying to see our way clear to spending more time together. Three weeks or a month over the holiday season would be a start. Time between now and then would pass quickly, I hoped. And on the strength of my recent exhibition at the Lasting Image Gallery, I'd been offered a spring show that would get me north again.

Though I'd called Veronica when I got back to let her know I was alright, she called a few days later. I'd been trying to settle into living alone and was still suffering from withdrawal. As well, the Muse had been playing hard to get, so I welcomed the sound of the phone ringing and any possible diversion.

"Hi guy," she said coyly. "Settling into life at the beach?"

"Hi yourself. I'm trying, but I must say that I miss you. How are you doing? Miss me yet?"

"I'm fine, but I started missing you when I left you at the airport." She paused, and I could hear her china teacup rattle against the saucer before she continued. "But I have exciting news that makes it all seem endurable."

"Do tell."

"First, I booked a flight, and my staff is going to cover me for a month. I'll be down mid-December—flying in on the twelfth and then back here January tenth. Almost a month, sweetheart. I can hardly wait."

"Wonderful! You'll be here in no time."

"And there's more. Remember the man at your exhibition who bought *Don Verde on Parade*?"

"Yes, I think I do. Irish descent. Rich. Middle-aged, good-looking, well-dressed. But I can't remember his name."

"Eric Connors. He's been in the art business forever. Made all his money in art. He retired a few years ago, but he told me recently that he's grown bored *attending* exhibitions, *buying* more art, and not really being personally involved. He's impressed with the work we've been exhibiting. He's taken a look at the books, and he would like me to consider taking him on as a working partner."

"Sounds like a fit, sweetie."

"So, if this works out with Connors, I'd like to explore the possibility of opening a small gallery near you. Say, in a hotel? I don't really know what I'm talking about, which is why I need to see the lay of the land. I only spent two weeks there with you, and we didn't trip around much."

"We can do that, for sure. In fact, I know a couple of hotel owners on the coast. We can go and visit them and see whether they think their guests might be interested in buying art."

"Perfect, Simon. I appreciate it."

"Hey, I might be benevolent, but I'm also doing it for selfish reasons too, dear heart."

"And for that I'm grateful, too."

"Send me the particulars of your arrival. I can't wait."

46.

ANTONIO AND NICK crouched over the coffee table, animated, talking about locations where they were going to plant the explosives, rhyming off street names. Marco had been swimming and walked in on them; he tried to make sense of what they were saying. They didn't notice him and continued talking.

When he realized what they were planning, he had to speak. "You guys are nuts. I'm fed up with you and your maniacal plan, Antonio. You're going to end up in prison," he said, tossing his towel over a chair, and turning away to walk outside. They stopped talking until he was out of the room and then continued.

Marco didn't expect that the strength or the sincerity of his words meant anything to them, but when he piled into their boat the next morning with two suitcases, he did expect that they had understood how he felt about their shenanigans.

He had become more involved with Sylvia and had been spending more and more time at the hacienda, each time depositing more of his clothes and belongings, until he was virtually moved in. He had a suite of rooms in the south wing of the house, with a balcony and access from the staircase that led to the patio. The women didn't appear to mind his presence. They all knew that he and Sylvia were close, that they spent a lot of time together, but he didn't think they suspected any romance between them. What did it matter anyway?

One evening, when they'd returned from paddling on the lake, Marco was tying up the boat while Sylvia had gone ahead. As he approached the shoreline, he saw that she was removing her clothes. Her arms extended, then she dipped silently into the water.

"Come and join me," she said quietly so her voice wouldn't carry across the still water. He kicked off his shoes, stripped, and followed her. The water temperature was higher than the evening air; he slipped into its enveloping warmth. They swam silently, apart from each other. Sylvia's rowing regime had also made her a strong swimmer. She did the breaststroke for several metres out into the middle of the lake. Stars studded the sky, and a waning moon provided enough light for Marco to see that she was resting, floating on her back, her arms stretched out behind her to maximize her buoyancy. Her small, perfect breasts glistened in the pale light. He swam over to her, then flipped on his back and floated beside her. Their hands touched, grasped, then held. They kissed and tried to embrace, but it was too difficult to stay afloat.

Sylvia giggled. "Let's go back now. Race you," she said and kicked off in a wicked butterfly stroke that propelled her away from him. He was no competition for her and made it back in his own dog-paddling time. She treaded water and waited for him, out from the shoreline, where the water was still deep. He caught up with her, winded. She was like a mermaid, her legs undulating beneath her; effortlessly, she stayed upright in the water. She cupped his face with her hands and kissed him, slowly, her lips caressing his with a passion he'd never experienced with her before. Her tongue sought his, and their mouths fused hungrily.

They splashed through the water until they could stand. She wrapped her legs around his waist and her arms around his shoulders. He carried her light slippery body ashore.

"I've got some towels in my room. Shall I carry you there?"

She kissed the nape of his neck and murmured, "Yes, please," in his ear. With her still holding onto him, he leaned down and scooped up their shoes and abandoned clothes. They moved soundlessly up the stairs to his wing of the house. When they reached the door, he turned the handle and carried her over the threshold.

He set her gently on his bed and went for towels. He brought three, one to wrap her hair in, and two for each of them to dry off. He patted her skin while she watched him, smiling coyly, he thought. "Here, let me dry you."

She stood up, and after she had fashioned a turban around her head, she took the other towel and proceeded to dry him gently, carefully, thoroughly. They dropped the damp towels on the floor while they lowered themselves onto the bed, succumbing to smouldering sexual energy, loving until they collapsed, exhausted. She was still asleep beside him when he opened his eyes the next morning. But Isabella was also there, standing at the foot of the bed, smiling and nodding, even approving, it seemed. She disappeared when Sylvia opened her eyes.

Sylvia smiled and leaned over to kiss him. She reached for his hand, turned it over, and looked at it closely. She stroked the perforations, long healed but visible in the meaty part between his index finger and thumb. "How did you get those?" she asked.

"Those were inflicted with a fork," he said, as he caressed her face with his other hand. "My wife was a tiny but powerful woman."

Sylvia kissed the scars.

"Would you like to kiss them all for me?" Marco said, smiling shyly. "It was dark when we came to bed and we didn't have a light on. You wouldn't have seen them all."

"There are more?"

Marco took her hand to his head and set her fingers along the rope of scar tissue. "That was the last one, when she threw a vase at me." Further along his skull he located another. "This one was a couple of years ago when she knocked me out with an iron skillet." He rolled on his stomach and raised his right hand to his left shoulder where there was an older, round scar on his shoulder. "This is where she bit me."

He rolled on his back again and reached for her. "Like you said, bruises fade. The pain is gone, but my body is a road map of scars that tell the story."

She looked in his eyes and kissed him gently on the cheek. "We shouldn't get lost then, with your road map and mine."

47.

ANTONIO AND NICK were floating in the pool on inflatable chairs, attempting to keep cool. The shade beneath the towering Ceiba provided some relief; otherwise, the sun was brutal.

Antonio was trying to keep his newspaper out of the water. "A house down the street from where your buddy lives is for rent. Close to where William Walker lived," Antonio said, looking up from the classified ads. He sipped his beer and thought for a long while. "I think we should rent it and see what we can do."

Nick and Antonio motored across the lake after breakfast the following morning. They tied up in the slip and walked a couple of blocks to the real estate office that was handling the rental of the house.

"I'm familiar with the interior of the house—I had a friend whose family lived there, so we don't need a tour. Save you some time," Antonio said to the agent. So, while Nick waited in the air-conditioned reception area devouring a current copy of *Time* magazine, Antonio signed the lease and paid the first and last month's rent in cash.

The agent drove them over to the house, opened the door for them, and followed them through as they inspected it. "Just as I remember it," Antonio said, smiling, as though he was fondly reflecting on times he'd spent there. The rental agent returned his smile and handed Antonio the keys. They shook hands once again before he left Nick and Antonio to their new house.

"Didn't know you knew someone who lived here," Nick said.

"I don't. Nor am I César Sanchez who signed the lease. Good to have another set of ID for times like these." Antonio grinned and looked around. The house was sparsely furnished save for stained mattresses on frame beds in two small bedrooms and a kitchen table and a couple of chairs. He unlocked the back door to an overgrown walled garden with small, uncomfortable-looking chairs set by a round iron table blistered with rust. A tiny shed that was unlocked appeared to have nothing more than some tools in it. They walked back into the kitchen. Nick moved the table and chairs away from a carpet that lay beneath, then pulled the carpet aside.

"Dead giveaway," Nick chuckled. "Not a carpet in any other part of the house, except here, hiding the trap door." An iron ring was set into one of the floor planks. He yanked on it. "Got anything I can tap this with, Tony? It's rusted or corroded."

Antonio went to the shed and returned with a hammer. Nick tapped the edges of the ring, the top, and all around again. He set the hammer on the floor and pulled the ring. This time the door reluctantly rose up from the floor. It was dark below. "Guess we don't have a flashlight, huh?"

"Now that we know the trap door is here, why don't we lock up," Antonio suggested. "I'll go to the power company, register, and pay the deposit. That'll get the lights turned on. But that probably won't happen until tomorrow. Then we can come back and see what's what."

Nick nodded in agreement. "I'll print off a layout of the streets around here and we can flesh out what we know about the houses. This is kind of fun. A bit like what we used to do in the Marines, but we aren't going to kill anyone."

48.

MARIA INHERITED my double bed as an early Christmas present. I bought a king-size, and the day it was to be delivered, I disassembled my old bed and began moving furniture around to accommodate the new one. When the truck came and I saw that mine was the only piece of cargo they were carrying, I hired them to haul Maria's new bed to her house, and she went with them. When she returned, I asked her to prepare the guest room, but that my *novia* would probably sleep with me. She blushed and giggled at our little conspiracy.

Novia is an ambiguous term that means girlfriend. Ticos tend to use the word *novia* instead of "lover," like North Americans would. To Ticos, *amante* or "lover" is akin to prostitute. And in the context of a wedding, the *novia* is the bride. In my case, since Veronica and I were not teenagers, nor were we getting married in the foreseeable future, we were *novio y novia* in the context of a strong romantic relationship.

The day before Veronica was due to arrive, I drove to Liberia and booked in at the Casa de Papel, where I would stay for the night and get out early the next morning to buy linens for the new bed and some canned goods—all the things I couldn't get in my neighbourhood. I was the only guest the first night I was there, and after I'd unpacked, I floated in the pool and cooled off from the drive. I had a new car, a used Subaru, and it had air conditioning, but still, Liberia was several degrees hotter because it was inland with no relief from the offshore breezes. When I got out of the car, the humidity assaulted me like a balloon filled with hot air exploding in my face.

I dressed and walked to a pizzeria that had been recommended to me. The wood ovens were in the corner of the main dining room. The pizza was the best I had tasted in a long time, and the slightly chilled red wine was wonderful. I chatted with the owner who asked where I was from. When I told him I owned a hacienda on the beach north of Playa Tamarindo, he asked if I'd heard about the body they'd found there last year. I told him I owned the house and had found the body. Fortunately, my pizza arrived, as did more customers; he left me to eat in peace, though I expect he was itching to learn more. But there wasn't much more to tell. He'd probably read *La Nación,* too.

Veronica's plane arrived on time, and as we drove away in air-conditioned comfort, I turned the opposite way she had anticipated. "I thought you lived north of here."

"That's right. But I came in last night and stayed at a lovely old place. I thought we could stay the night there and visit a couple resorts farther down the coast while we were here."

"Great idea, Simon. A true busman's holiday." We pulled up outside Casa de Papel and I got her luggage out of the trunk. "Beautiful place," Veronica said as she stepped out of the car.

"And," I said, "it has a small pool in the garden."

The owner met us, and I introduced him to Veronica. He gave me my key, and we went inside. She tossed her purse on a chair, and we folded into each other's arms. A kiss that began tenderly evolved into hungry passion. "Maybe we can put off the swim until later?" I said breathlessly and led her to the bed where we fell into a bubbling cauldron of lovemaking.

The following morning after breakfast we checked out of Casa de Papel and headed in a southwesterly direction, towards my place, but we would continue on further south, beyond Playa Tamarindo where there was a little hook of headland. Nestled in a bay on Playa Langosta, Victor Ramirez had built Cala Luna Boutique Hotel and Villas where the rooms started at somewhere around three hundred dollars a night. My assumption was that if the guests had as much taste as they did money, perhaps they might buy art. Victor and I had met last year at a civic function in Tamarindo, and he offered me a standing invitation to visit, so I didn't feel out of line when we arrived unannounced.

The entrance to the resort was elegant yet understated—its architecture integrated with the local flora. As we neared the hotel, the ambiance welcomed us like a gracious host. We parked and entered a foyer where water trickled over a moss-covered wall. Through floor-to-ceiling windows in the lounge we could see an infinity pool and the ocean beyond. A pretty Tica smiled at us when we walked up to the reception desk.

"Good morning. How can I help you?" she asked in flawless English.

"We're looking for Victor Ramirez. We don't have an appointment, but if you would be so kind as to give him my card, perhaps he will remember me." She took the card and disappeared for a few moments. When she returned, Victor was walking behind her.

"Well, well. Simon Patrick. What a pleasant surprise." Victor shook my hand and patted me on the back.

"Good to see you again, Victor. I'd like you to meet my *novia*, Veronica Masters." He took her hand and kissed her on the cheek.

"Very good to meet you, Señorita Masters. Welcome to Cala Luna. Come. Come and sit down." We chose a table overlooking the infinity pool. "Is there anything I can offer you? A drink? Coffee perhaps?"

"Thanks, Victor. We'll probably stay for lunch, so we'll wait. Actually, it's Veronica who might have a proposition for you. She owns a successful gallery in New York. I just had a sellout show there."

"Interesting. Very interesting. I'd like to hear about it, but..." He saw Veronica open her tablet. He looked at his watch. "I am sorry, but I have a meeting that starts in ten minutes. What do you say we meet for lunch, and I can hear more about your proposition then, Veronica?"

We had an hour to kill before lunch, so we bought a couple of bottles of water at the gift shop and toured the manicured grounds. The grass was like a soft cushion under our feet. The exercise room was occupied with glistening bodies that looked toned and taut. Other specimens of the glamorous side of humanity lounged in the sun next to the pool where more svelte bodies floated or did lazy, languid laps. We kicked off our sandals and walked along the beach. People lay splayed beneath umbrellas, others surfed in the crashing waves. The sun was hot, but the breeze was forgiving.

Veronica's presentation was impressive—not only to me, but to Victor whose expression was one of delight. Beneath that, one could almost see the wheels turning as he considered the fiscal possibilities. And when she brought up my work, he giggled like a little boy.

"These are wonderful, Simon," he blurted. "I can see them hanging here in my hotel. The guests would love them."

"Do you think they'd buy them?" I asked for Veronica.

"I am almost certain, Simon. We have people from all over the world, and they spend a lot of money, as you know. We could hang a show, publicize it well, and see what happens. That way, we can do some market research before we lay out money for a proper gallery. What do you think?" He looked at me, then at Veronica.

"It sounds like a sensible approach to me," I said. I looked at Veronica.

"Yes. It'd be great to test the market during the high season to see if Cala Luna could support a small gallery. Perhaps we could also carry artistic wearable creations and accessories. It would be fun to research the area for talent." Veronica smiled at Victor. "When do you think would be a suitable time, Victor?"

"Well, we're just heading into the Christmas season, during

which time the place is totally booked. A lot of families—often three generations of them, so I don't think then would be a suitable time. What about February? That's well before spring break when we're inundated with young Americans using their parents' credit cards. Not art buyers, really."

"What do you think, Simon? If we're featuring your work, does that give you enough time to do, say, ten paintings?"

"I've done a couple since I've been back. I had four that I didn't take up to the show in New York, so that's six. Sure, four paintings in the next six weeks is doable."

49.

THE FASHION SHOW was set for December 28. Twenty ensembles would be modelled: several with wraparound skirts and gauzy bikini cover-ups. Others were three pieces: skirt and blouse, and Capri pants and blouse, over which the models draped shawls of matching colours. Some of their customers would model outfits they'd already purchased. Posters had been printed and two weeks before the show—a week before Christmas—they would be distributed from Laguna de Apoyo, to Catarina, and to Granada and all the towns in-between. They were producing a tape recording that would be broadcast through the speaker of a car they would hire to drive around populated areas, encouraging people to attend and to start the New Year off with a special outfit.

Marco and Sylvia were no longer trying to keep their relationship a secret; the tension of posturing, of keeping their distance when they were around others, all that pretence was dropped. They openly hugged and nuzzled no matter who was around to see them. Sylvia kept her room down the hall, but she slept in Marco's. She'd never felt so calm and at the same time electrified with a man. She could barely remember her husband behind the total eclipse that was Marco Vincente Alvarez Soto.

Sylvia had always been a confident woman, but now she dared to dream. She felt inspired. She looked around her, where she was, how she was living, and it was as if she'd been blind and was now sighted. She was excited about the fashion show. *VIVA*, a virtual magazine published in Granada, had called and asked if they could do a preview and an interview for their December edition. Who knew if anything would come of it, but it was worth trying.

While she was impressed with the media's interest, she was a bit concerned about the success of the publicity and the possibility of the women's husbands being alerted. Marco had assured her that he would hire extra guards for the evening who would discreetly screen the people entering the grounds. She wouldn't tell the reporter who the women were or the circumstances that had brought them together. Or should she?

50.

THE TUNNEL WAS NARROW, so they had to crouch, poking ahead of them with brooms to clear the cobwebs and urge the resident rats to lead the way. In the brief time that the slaves had been under Walker's tyrannical rule, driven by their desperate desire to be free again, they had managed to dig two tunnels that were, in total, almost three blocks long: one in the direction of the bank, and the other toward the lake. In two weeks, Antonio and Nick had pushed through the tunnels that originated from the house they were renting, and presumably, from Walker's cellar. The bank was further down the street. They bought a spool of wire, sockets, and bulbs so as to light the passageway from power in the rented house. The slaves had been ingenious; they'd reinforced the tunnels with ribs of iron, probably the work of a fellow blacksmith. The walls of the tunnels were strapped in places, and above the strapping, they'd driven bamboo tubes into the earth that reached up to street level, for air. They'd even whitewashed the ceilings in some of them, to reflect the light from the lanterns or candles they would have toted. And almost one hundred and sixty years later it was still intact—the walls firm despite hundreds of rainy seasons and the odd tremor.

In one of the final legs of tunnels, someone had written "*Libertad*" and an arrow. There was a street named Libertad, but presumably, this sign signified the direction to freedom. Sadly, they had never reached the lake or the freedom that it offered. The tunnel stopped abruptly.

Antonio walked along the street, pausing, like a gawking tourist, taking photographs of the convent and church, waiting to hear Nick's cap pistol pop under the street where he was making his way through the tunnel. Antonio followed the sound and determined how far along Nick was. They'd followed Calle El Arsenal from Walker's cellar westward and then ended a few metres short of Calle Atravesada. On one side of the street, Mi Museo, a ceramic museum, housed ancient pottery as well as the work of a contemporary co-operative. Banco LAFISE Bancentro was across from it. They mapped the route of the tunnels and measured the distance that they would need to reach their destination.

"When I go back through, I'll figure out how many modest little blasts we'll need; then I'll come back later, plant the explosives, and key their locations into my GPS," Nick explained. "We'll need a cellphone for each detonation. And I assure you, the blasts will be small. Luckily, the slaves thought to ventilate. I've got some buddies who are miners, and they'll give me some rubber mats to muffle the sound and keep the dust down. We'll need wheelbarrows and shovels, and we're going to get dirty, so keep a set of grubs at the house. Like you say, '*poco á poco,*' we'll blast a little at a time, over the course of the month of December, until we get beneath the bank." This kind of excavating was infinitely more efficient and faster than the slaves' digging and pawing, but also much slower than what normal U.S. Marines considered expedient.

"The explosions will be subtle, like subterranean thunder," Nick said. "I bet they won't be heard much above ground, especially with the fireworks and cannons blasting. But the best part of all is that I can detonate each sequence remotely. We can stand right over the area we're going to blast and hear for ourselves."

That night, when Nick went to bed, Consolación visited his dreams again. Though he was silent, he was smiling and seemed to be praising him. His arms were sweeping around his head. He danced a little jig. It was a pleasant, reassuring dream.

They started to hear the first volleys and blasts of fireworks at the end of November but waited until the tension built and with it more explosions. Tractor-trailers full of fireworks parked outside supermarkets throughout the city, enticing people to buy, and sooner or later, they would. It was in their blood.

Nick and Antonio's first blast was on December third, choreographed to coincide with the weekend's incessant explosions. Like most evenings, Calle El Arsenal was void of pedestrians. The touring carriages parked for the night, and the horses pastured in fields near the lake. Wise tourists took taxis after sunset to avoid being robbed, and Nicas were in their homes or guests in the homes of friends and family. "You could roll a cannonball down the middle of the street," Antonio joked.

Nick and Antonio ambled along past the corner of the street. Nick offered Antonio a cigarette, and they both leaned against one of the buildings across from where they'd planted the explosive. When one volley of fireworks blasted the night air, Nick looked at Antonio, nodded, flicked the cover of the new cellphone he'd purchased for the job. He'd rigged the phone so that when he keyed in the explosive's specific number, the electrical charge would be enough to create the explosion. The fireworks continued blasting long after Nick's blast.

"Felt a little like being over top of the metro in Mexico City. Just a little rumbling. Nothing else," Antonio said.

"When we come back tomorrow, we'll need to shovel the stuff that's been blown out, see how far we got. Do a little house cleaning. See that everything is still in place. A few more nights like this, and we're good to go, bro." Nick tossed his cigarette butt in the gutter. They flagged a taxi and directed the driver to the wharf where Antonio kept his boat.

51.

VERONICA WAS JAZZED about her meeting with Victor Ramirez at the Cala Luna, but now, I was taking her to another upscale place: The Four Seasons Resort Costa Rica. It was located on a cliff overlooking the ocean. It had no beachfront, but it did have three swimming pools, an Arnold Palmer designed eighteen-hole golf course, and a conference centre and ballroom, so it was a destination for people with disposable money.

I knew the manager and had called him before we set out. It was a dramatic setting; the views of the Pacific were spectacular. Gerardo Lopez met us at the front desk and took us on a tour.

"We've got our last conference in here before the Christmas season." Gerardo's arms swept around him like a windmill. "The place is fully booked until the eighteenth and then we get a short reprieve before guests start arriving for Christmas. Very little down time." He smiled confidently. "Would you like coffee? We can sit in the shade by the pool." He signalled for a waiter who nodded and promptly walked over and showed us to our table.

"We'd love some coffee and a chance to talk," I said. We all sat down and the waiter took our order. Once again, after my introduction, Veronica took the lead and opened the cover on her tablet. She told him her thoughts of mounting art shows and showed him the website of Lasting Image Gallery. Gerardo knew my work from attending one of my shows when he was in New York a few years ago, and had actually purchased a small canvas. But his eyes lit up when she clicked on my gallery within hers.

"I love the parrots, Simon," he said, laughing. "They're wonderful. You've really captured the vibrancy of the landscape. And the colours are stunning. Marvellous."

"Thank you, Gerardo. I've just returned from a successful exhibition at Veronica's gallery in New York. She's hoping that she can find a venue that would resonate with this kind of work, to open a small gallery on the premises of an already well-established hotel."

Gerardo's bushy eyebrows rose dramatically. "Is that so?"

"We'd start on a small scale with perhaps a couple of exhibitions a year. Carry a line of high-end accessories, perhaps some designer swimwear. That kind of thing," Veronica said. She sipped her coffee, and we were all silent for a moment.

"As you know, I am only the manager in this establishment," Gerardo said apologetically. "I would have to make a presentation to the principals. This would be a difficult time to get consensus from the four of them, what with Christmas and everything. One is in Los Angeles; another in Paris. The other two are in San José."

"We understand. No rush, Gerardo. We just wanted to take a look at the resort, propose our idea, see what you think, and to drink some of your fine coffee." I smiled at him and nodded at Veronica. We all rose, shook hands, and he walked us out to the car.

"It has been a delight to meet you, Veronica, and hear your interesting proposition," Gerardo said, bowing slightly. "Always a pleasure to see you, Simon, and keep painting those wonderful parrots. I have your cards. Give me some time, and I'll call you in the New Year. I promise."

52.

MARCO LOCATED THE OWNER of a bar in Catarina that had gone out of business and was able to rent all their patio furniture. He hired a lighting man from a theatre in Granada for the evening. The upstairs balcony was perfect; the lighting man could spotlight the models down the stairs and onto the runway that ran down the centre aisle of the tables. The runway was edged in strings of small LED lights that were unobtrusive, yet defined the walkway for the girls to move confidently.

The hacienda was brimming with energy, excitement, and enthusiasm. The feature had appeared in *VIVA*, and the phone rang constantly with inquiries and reservations. The magazine featured some stunning photographs of the models posing in their outfits beside sprays of bougainvillea, beneath the lipstick palms, and on the dock with the lake in the background. With two weeks left before the show, they had already sold forty tickets; there was seating for one hundred guests, and it seemed certain that they would fill the seats.

Christmas was almost an afterthought at the hacienda, but Yolanda prepared a feast, and the women decorated the patio with garlands. They exchanged gifts; Marco gave each of the women silver bracelets, including Sylvia, but when they went to bed that night a bouquet of red roses and baby's breath waited for her on the bureau, a bottle of champagne chilled in an ice bucket by the bed, and candles flickered in votive glasses. Marco guided Sylvia into the room. "How beautiful, Marco! It takes my breath away."

"I can honestly say exactly the same thing about you, my darling." He took one of the roses from the vase and held it out to her. Then, he knelt in front of her, removed the solitaire diamond that hung on one of the leaves, and held it up to her. "I love you, Sylvia. Will you marry me?"

A tear dropped on Marco's hand. "Yes, Marco. I love you, too. And yes, I will marry you." He rose and slid the diamond onto her finger, wrapped her in his arms, and held her tight. Isabella stood near them, smiling her approval.

The next morning, they lay together, sunlight filtering through the shuttered windows. Yolanda had brought them coffee, and they were enjoying the peacefulness of the early morning. Marco rose to open the terrace doors. He turned back to her. "I think we should go on a holiday after this show is over," he said, smiling. He sat down on the bed beside her. "What about San Andrés in Colombia? Have you ever been?"

"No. I've never been out of the country. Well, I almost made it as far the border once, but I was turned back because I didn't have a passport."

"Well, we'll make sure your papers are in order. When the aftermath of the show and the orders that will come from it are out of the way, we'll plan a getaway." They carried their coffee onto the balcony and sat at the table. He took her hands in his, then admired the ring on her finger. "I will be so proud to have you as my wife, Sylvia."

53.

WE ACCOMPLISHED what we'd set out to do. One hotel had booked an exhibition for February, and the second one looked promising. We had planted the seeds, and now we'd wait to see what germinated. At least, Veronica could wait. I couldn't. I had to paint, but that wasn't a big deal for me. I was inspired—the creative juices were bubbling. Veronica was Veronica. She gave me my space, but when I wasn't working, we frolicked in the waves, walked along the shoreline, and daydreamed about her future and mine, perhaps "our" future. Christmas was low-key; we lingered in the luxurious king-sized bed in the morning, followed by a leisurely breakfast, a swim, a sunset walk, dinner on the veranda, and finally, a fire on the beach. The flames were mesmerizing. We cuddled on the blanket, quiet, content.

"Now that you've set things in motion, and we still have a few weeks before you have to go back, is there anything you would like to do or see?" I stroked her hair and continued looking into the flames. She took a while to answer. "Is it far to Granada, Nicaragua?"

"A few hours. Depends on the border. Would you like to go there?"

"A colleague was there last winter and showed me pottery and textile work she'd brought back. The architecture is so different, so colonial. Some of it European. It looks fascinating. It's a city I would love to visit."

"We can go there, for sure. I haven't been there either."

The next morning while we drank coffee, Veronica surfed the internet for places to stay in Granada, and sights to see in the surrounding area. In one of her searches, *VIVA*, a fashion magazine, popped up. Veronica audibly salivated over some of the photographs.

"Laguna de Apoyo is a crater lake outside of Granada," she read. "There's going to be a fashion show there in a couple of days. The pieces look fabulous—swimwear ensembles. It's exactly what I'm looking for. Think we can make it?"

"If we leave early tomorrow morning."

54.

THEY WERE ON SCHEDULE. They'd blasted all the way down the street to the wall of the bank's basement. It seemed to take them forever to clean out the silt and sand as it had to be done in the cover of darkness with a truck they'd rented from a friend of Nick's. Each night, they loaded bags of it and trucked it to a farm outside Granada. But they got it done, and they still had to wait a week for Christmas and the ensuing pyrotechnics to mask and muffle the next phase of their project.

Nick had been amazed by the accuracy of Antonio's grandmother, had been talking about her so much that Antonio drove up to Masaya for him to meet her. They'd spent the day with her, listening to her tales. *Abuela* had been a widow since Antonio was a young boy. She'd lived alone for all those years, save when Antonio stayed with her during the war. She had lots of friends in her neighbourhood, and at the age of ninety-three, she continued to entertain. She'd been a wonderful cook in her day but didn't prepare many dishes anymore; she ordered in from a *comedor*—a glorified food stall with a couple of tables for customers—and the cook's son delivered her orders on his moto. When her grandson had arrived with his friend, she turned on her cellphone, pressed a number—obviously on speed-dial—and placed an order for fried chicken, tortillas, and a half a dozen bottles of Victoria beer. She sipped rum that she kept in the freezer, and as the day wore on, her accounts became more animated. *Abuela* told the boys stories that she'd heard as a little girl, including accounts of the slaves as well as the tunnel. She spoke in Spanish, embellished here and there with some Indian dialect that Antonio had never mastered. Nick still didn't speak much more than restaurant Spanish, so Antonio had to translate while *Abuela* waited, graciously patient, nodding and smiling. When she'd gotten to the story about her uncle Augusto Sandino, he was glad that Nick didn't understand, that he was able to dilute the victorious battle. No doubt, if Nick knew about that battle, it would be a gringo version that included neither defeat nor retreat. Nick appeared moved by her animated and often horrid accounts about the brutal treatment of the slaves. Stories that had been told and retold from her elders, passed down to her.

She made clacking noises with her mouth and patted her legs for sound effects when she told of the hooded skeleton that drove a cart through the streets, its wheels creaking, the horses' hooves clattering on cobblestones. Nick's eyes widened, saucer-like, while he listened to his dream being recounted.

It was dusk. They had driven back to Granada as the sun was beginning to set, staining the land shades of rose. They'd crossed the lake silently within that rosy glow, the city's skyline a backlit silhouette. When they got to the house, Antonio switched on the flat screen and flopped in his chair.

"I wonder if any of the descendants are still living around here," Nick mused. He was lying on the sofa, seemingly mesmerized by the channels flicking across the screen. "I'd like to pay them back for the transgressions of one of my despicable countrymen, the sick little bastard."

"I would imagine so. Like the old saying, 'We are all related.'"

"If their ancestors were slaves, I couldn't imagine them being in the upper echelons of society today, poor beggars. Wouldn't it be a blast to be able to give them some of the spoils?"

"Blast being the operative word, Nicko."

Earlier in the week, Antonio had been to Banco LAFISE Bancentro. He told an attendant that he wanted to visit his safety deposit box. An officious-looking man in a shiny black suit that was too small for him appeared, rattling a ring of keys. He unlocked the door to the stairwell and walked ahead of Antonio who was squeezing a flat playdough-like material in his hand as he followed.

Near the door to the room where the safety deposit boxes were, Antonio tripped. He broke his fall by reaching for the door jamb, where he slapped an all but invisible piece of C-4 plastic explosive. The attendant hadn't noticed. He entered the room, and after the man solemnly inserted the bank's key, Antonio turned his own key in the lock, pulled out his safety deposit box, and smiled at the attendant, who got the message and closed the door behind him. Antonio pawed through some of the documents he stored there, killing time, and after he thought sufficient time had passed, opened the door. "You can lock up now, please."

"Will that be everything for today, sir?" the attendant asked as they headed for the stairs.

"I think that's all. Thank you." The attendant opened the door and, as if he were reluctant to leave, Antonio looked back at the room of safety deposit boxes. He could see nothing on the door jamb. They climbed the stairs and as he was about to leave, he asked, "Will the ATM be operating through the Christmas holidays?"

"Only until six p.m. on Christmas Eve, sir. Then it will be open again on Christmas Day morning."

"Thank you. I'll remember that. Merry Christmas." The ATM and the bank were normally guarded, but that night, after six, as he thought he remembered from previous years, the guards would be home eating tamales with their families.

As Antonio had learned, Nick knew his way around the shadier side of life in Nicaragua. His military background made him wary, suspecting, and often paranoid, but his training had honed his eyes and all of his senses to read situations and characters. He had several contacts in the expat community, some with criminal backgrounds. In November, when one of them was moving to Panama, he'd had a kind of brotherhood garage sale. Nick had rummaged through his buddy's memorabilia, bought a Bowie knife and a couple of punches that were designed to pop the locks on safety deposit boxes. He'd use one of them, keep the other for backup, and Antonio would come along behind him and bag the contents. He'd found a website that explained the tools of the burglary trade—it was all on the internet. He read that a lock could be punched in five seconds. Even if it took ten seconds, he could do close to two hundred boxes in a little over a half-hour, with Antonio gathering up the spoils. Maybe they'd only do half of the boxes. Hell, who knew what was in them? Maybe they'd have to fence some of the stuff and that would take work and create a trail. They'd leave a wheelbarrow in the tunnel and ferry the loot back to the house off Calle El Arsenal.

"So, what are our plans once we get back to the house, Tony?"

Antonio had just returned from the city and they were cooling off in the pool. He didn't answer for a couple of minutes. He finally turned to look at Nick, and said, "My thought is to stow the stuff in several suitcases. I'll book the plane with Hector to take us away for a few days. My grandmother mentioned that my uncle's farm is vacant."

"Rural is good. What about Ometepe? There are some decent hotels there."

"On an island over Christmas and New Year's? Forget it. Let me think about it for a while."

"Don't take too long, buddy. Time's a-wasting."

55.

I WATCHED FROM A ROOFTOP *down the street from where Antonio and Nick were doing their work. The season was in their favour—the endless blasting was akin to a festive war zone with Granada under siege. Police cruisers circled like sharks on elusive prey. On a rooftop across the street from me, a marimba band was set up at one end of an expansive terrace, the sensuous rhythms propelling couples across the dance floor. Women in colourful dresses swirled, their laughter ringing in the night air. Beyond the dance floor, people grazed and chatted along a banquet table. Others mingled in front of the bar. At the far end of the terrace, men were lighting fireworks; rainbows of colour blasted through the darkness, its ashy remnants cascading till spent, except for one large ember that no one noticed. It lodged on a ledge and settled in a crevice where it was protected by the building.*

I watched as the glowing ember enveloped dry leaves and bougainvillea petals, fanned by a gentle breeze off the lake. The ember grew stronger; a flame ignited and licked the area around it like a snake hungrily probing the air. It found the caña de India, *and in no time the dry cane that strapped the ceilings beneath the rooftops caught, and bright red flames shot out from the building. Women screamed; cellphones were engaged, numbers called. The band members gathered their instruments and huddled in a corner, anxious to leave the hysterical party guests who were leaning over the railings, calling for help.*

Sirens eventually screamed their approach, growing louder, stopping abruptly outside the building. Ladders were raised, climbed, and water shot from hoses. The flames were extinguished, leaving smoke and steam to cloud the air. Firefighters had entered the house and climbed two floors to the terrace where they coaxed the party down the smoke-filled staircase.

Police arrived and secured the area for a couple of blocks on either side of Calle El Arsenal. They questioned the guests, took notes, and determined the cause of the fire. The crowd ultimately dispersed, and the officers returned to their cruisers to find that the tires of all four cars were flatter than the pavement on which they were parked.

56.

THE MEDIA COVERAGE for the fashion show had been excellent, and all the tickets sold. Yolanda had been making canapés and freezing them to reheat that evening. Marco had rented glasses and purchased wine, mineral water, and various juices. He'd also hired Yolanda's teenage son and his friend to serve, even supplying them with white shirts and black pants. As long as they didn't come in their bare feet, they'd be fine. And even if they did, it wouldn't matter.

Marco had also strung lights and planted floodlights in the gardens to add more drama to what would be a beautifully lit show. Each night after dinner, the women sat on the patio and watched, offering encouragement and comments as Marco made adjustments. Tomorrow night, the models and the lighting man would come for a dress rehearsal and walk-through. The dresses and ensembles hung in the bedroom that had become a dressing room, patiently awaiting bodies to bring them to life.

Sylvia looked over the names on the guest list. There were familiar Nicaraguan names; a couple were coming from Costa Rica, gringos, judging from their names. The women looked for their family names but found none. She felt confident that Marco was as good as his word on providing a doorman to screen people who entered, just to be sure. The women didn't seem concerned, but anything could happen.

On the morning of the rehearsal, Marco was drinking coffee on the balcony off his bedroom. Their bedroom, he thought and smiled. Sylvia was already up and at work. She'd brought him a carafe of coffee, the daily newspaper folded beside it, and before she left, she planted a noisy kiss on his cheek. When he opened the paper, he didn't need to read the article to know that Antonio and Nick had followed through with their Christmas Eve heist. A bank's chamber of safety deposit boxes had been emptied after the door was detonated by a bomb. Further investigation discovered a tunnel that led to the oldest house in town, the nineteenth-century home of William Walker. The house next to it had been rented but was now vacated. There was no sign of the suspects, though Granada was being searched high and low for a man named César Sanchez, which, Marco knew, was one of Antonio's personas. They'd used either the boat or the plane to make their getaway, and for sure it wouldn't be to Antonio's house, Marco thought. Idiots! If they were smart, they'd be far away from Granada and stay away for a good long time. He threw the paper on the table and went downstairs.

57.

WE CHECKED IN at a small boutique hotel on Calle El Consulado. It had indoor parking and a pool; the latter we soon learned was a prerequisite for attempting to stay cool in Granada. Veronica had been like a little girl with her face pressed against the window as we drove north, soaking in all the flora and fauna, exclaiming when she saw horses tethered along the roadsides. "Such handsome lawn mowers," she said. Enormous wind turbines turned lazily along the shores of Lake Nicaragua. When we got to Granada, she almost burst with enthusiasm. We had a quick dip in the pool, dressed, and then headed east in the breeze that was coming off the lake.

"What a lovely city," she remarked as we crossed the street, walking in front of the horses parked with their carriages at Parque Central. Vendors lined the north side of the park, displaying pottery, leather, and textile crafts. "Oh, my, this is going to be fun," she said before she disappeared.

I elected to sit on a bench and watch the scenery as she browsed through the stalls. She eventually returned with an embroidered bag, a sarong-like dress, and a couple of handsome pieces of pottery. "It's beautiful work. I can see this in a gallery gift shop," she said, turning the vase around in her hands. "And now, I can hardly wait to see the creations at the fashion show."

We spent the rest of the day sightseeing, took a walk down to the lake, had an iced latte at a restaurant on Calle La Calzada, and visited the cathedral that was a landmark on the central plaza. We ate pecan waffles at Kathy's Waffle House and watched policemen wrap crime-scene tape over the door of a house down the street, on Calle El Arsenal. Residents were outside their homes watching, no doubt speculating on the neighbourhood investigation. I'd read of the robbery in the paper while I was waiting for Veronica. Impressive. The man renting the house had fled without a trace. We walked down the street and saw the bank that had been robbed, draped with more crime-scene tape.

Luckily, we'd only planned to stay in Granada for one night. While there was air conditioning in our beautifully decorated room, the stately old city was jittery with the presence of police. No doubt customers who had safety deposit boxes were furious, anxious about their stolen jewels, money, and documents. The police investigation had tainted the atmosphere, and we looked forward to leaving the next day. We made the best of our evening and dined at the Hotel Alhambra where we drank wine and watched the activities in the park. Lovers took advantage of dimly lit areas beneath trees to kiss, caress, and fondle. Families strolled along the sidewalks, parents watching their wee ones run ahead to meet other toddlers. It was calm and relatively cool after sundown. We lingered over coffee then hired a carriage to take us down the street to our hotel.

We got up early the next morning and left after breakfast. Traffic was light; buses, horses, and wagons led by yokes of oxen moved at their own pace, and we didn't challenge them. We were in no hurry. The temperature dropped dramatically as we left the city of Granada and climbed into the mountains. Veronica had found a resort with cabins, and after we got some groceries and refreshments, that's where we headed.

"I read that motorized boats are prohibited on this lake," Veronica recalled. "The Indigenous people own and operate all of the resorts here. Impressive." And it was.

The cabin was a short distance to the shoreline where there

was a sandy beach with a couple of windsurf boards at rest. The silence was profound, save for the birds that called and sang from the canopy, and the intermittent choruses of cicadas winding up for the heat of the day. It was tranquil bliss that we soaked up for the entire day as we swam, tried to windsurf, and had a late lunch in our resort's dining room.

The fashion show was exquisite—and that's even by sometimes snobby New Yorkers' standards. The hacienda was a stunning, rambling place with well-kept gardens. We were asked to arrive just before sunset, which in this part of the world is about six o'clock, and that enabled us to enjoy the surroundings. We walked down to the dock to look at the view from this side of the lake and tried to find our cabin.

With the natural sunset came a gentle wash of floodlights that illuminated the palms and ferns and bougainvillea, which provided a colourful backdrop. A trio of musicians played Latin rhythms, and when everyone had been served wine and canapés, the music faded slightly. A spotlight then washed over the first model. It followed her as she strode down the stairs and onto the runway as the musicians struck up a lively, sun-soaked sequence of guitar riffs. The response was enthusiastic with women and men all applauding. Veronica snapped shots of the models and took some notes as each of them approached our table. The outfits were bright and colourful, the fabric moved and swayed as the women sashayed along the runway. Shawls were removed to exhibit Capri pants and tops; wraparound skirts snapped open to reveal bikinis in a tastefully modest striptease. By the end of the show, Veronica had photographed the majority of the ensembles. We waited for the stampede to thin before we spoke again to Sylvia Mendoza, the organizer of the event. She greeted us when we arrived, and when Veronica explained her idea, she asked that we remain so that she could speak to us with fewer distractions. Women were upstairs trying on the sample garments; others were making appointments for fittings and placing orders for outfits. A young man brought us coffee, and a few minutes later Sylvia Mendoza joined us at our table.

"You must be thrilled with the evening, Sylvia," Veronica said.

"I really am," she agreed. "And now the work begins with sewing all the orders." She laughed. "Clearly though, I'm delighted. We have a line, as you call it."

"And I'm really impressed with it all," Veronica told her. "I mentioned briefly before the show that I was in the midst of setting up a gallery and gift shop at a resort on the west coast in Costa Rica. I'd like to sell some pieces like yours—in perhaps three different sizes. I'm not looking for a lot of stock—just a few shawls and accessories. I love the jewellery the women were wearing tonight. Was it yours?"

"Well, yes, I chose it. A woman in Granada makes it, and she lent it to me for the show. I'm sure she'd be interested in your shop. Actually, there's another woman who makes colourful clay beads. I have some of her work, too. We just didn't use it tonight."

"We're going to be here for another night, right Simon?" Veronica asked, looking for confirmation. I nodded, and she continued. "I took shots of everything I liked tonight, which was most, I must say. I also made notes, and I have your price list. If you're free some time tomorrow, I can come back with an order. I want to spend some time thinking about numbers, and what will sell in a season."

"Why don't you both come by for lunch tomorrow? I think everything will be cleaned up by then, and my head will be a bit clearer."

"After this show, I am surprised you're still standing. Lunch sounds great," Veronica said. "In the meantime, get some rest, contented with the fact that you had a fabulous show. Well done." The women shook hands and brushed cheeks.

I shook Sylvia's hand, murmured my thanks, and we were off. Things were falling into place.

58.

HECTOR HAD FLOWN THEM to a ranch Antonio's great-uncle owned on the Río Escondido where he had lived until recently, when, according to Antonio's grandmother, he'd fallen off his horse and broken his leg. He was convalescing with his daughter in Masaya, not far from *Abuela*. The farm was fairly isolated, it had a good well, there were fish in the river, and the house was secure, clean, and comfortable. When they'd unloaded the four suitcases and supplies, they wished Hector a safe flight back. After he'd motored out into the water and lifted off, they waved with both their hands in the air, then giggled, giddily, like children on Christmas morning.

Their net was an assortment of American dollars, gold bars, raw and cut gems, jewellery, medals, and old coins. They hadn't counted the dollars, but the pile continued to grow as they emptied the suitcases into the middle of the *sala* where they sat on the highly polished mahogany floor, sifting through the contents like little boys in a sandbox full of toy cars. The individual mountains of jewellery and medals, bills and coins grew, toppling and expanding in their growing surface on the floor.

"I count three hundred thousand American," Nick said after wrapping elastics around several bundles of cash. "I have no idea what antique coins are worth, but some of them look ancient. And the gold? That's going to fetch, let's see, with two bars at a kilo a piece, I'd say around eighty grand. Plus, with all the jewellery and loose gems, I bet we're looking at a couple of million in total, bro."

"The money is easy enough to deal with; it's the coins and jewelery that we have to sell," Antonio said.

"I've got some friends," Nick said. "Should be easy enough. Just have to be careful."

Antonio looked at Nick and then at the spoils. "Can I make a suggestion, Nick?"

"What's that?"

"That we put all the documents together in an envelope addressed to Banco LAFISE Bancentro and have Hector drop it in the night deposit, if they have one, or mail it. We don't need to complicate people's lives further by destroying their documents. However, we don't know the provenance of the gold and jewels either; there's a good chance they were previously acquired through questionable means. We're just going to redistribute the wealth, make a few people happy."

"I'm with you there, Tony. No need to tip the scales in the karma department."

They separated all of the spoils and stashed bags beneath beams, under floorboards, and in a false back his great-uncle had carved in an armoire. He also knew of a similar cache upstairs under a bureau where his great-aunt had kept her money and the few gems she had owned.

Nick and Antonio took care of business, and then celebrated.

59.

WHEN VERONICA AND I went to Sylvia's for lunch, a man was in the driveway, locking his car. Marco introduced himself as Sylvia's fiancé and led us into the house. The seating for the show had been dismantled and stowed away. We sat on the patio at a glass-covered wrought-iron table on chairs that were covered in colourful cushions. Yolanda brought a carafe of sangria and poured.

Marco took his glass and raised it in our direction. "I welcome you both to Laguna de Apoyo once again, and I toast the new relationship you have with Sylvia. *Felicidades*."

"*Felicidades*," we responded.

After we had a sip and nibbled on some of the trout paté and crackers, Veronica pulled out her tablet. "I thought you might like to see my gallery in New York," she began.

They pulled their chairs closer to Veronica's and watched as she typed in the URL for the Lasting Image Gallery. They leaned in closer, both obviously interested.

"And this is the work that Simon does. He had a sellout exhibition there in October. These were the pieces." She opened the gallery with my work. I enjoyed watching people respond to Don Verde, and Sylvia didn't disappoint me with her bubbly laughter.

"He's wonderful, Simon. So comical," she said. She looked over at Marco to see what he thought of them. His face was drawn, and he appeared to be wincing in pain. "Are you alright,

Marco?" She put her hand to his forehead.

"It's nothing. Just a slight headache. I must be allergic to some pollen now. I'll go up and take an antihistamine." Marco rose quickly, noisily scraping the chair against the tiles.

We continued talking. Sylvia and Veronica appeared to be getting on well. I was enjoying myself. The sangria was refreshing. When Yolanda brought the gazpacho, she whispered in Sylvia's ear.

"Marco sends his regrets," Sylvia explained. "Apparently, his headache has developed into a migraine. He hopes to see you again soon and says he's terribly sorry."

"Nothing to be sorry about, at all. Migraines can be crippling," I said. Thankfully, I had never had one but my first wife was often stricken with them and needed to be in a dark room for what I remember were days on end.

"Anyway, the gazpacho is wonderful. And the panino is delicious," Veronica told Sylvia.

"Thank you. I'll be sure to tell Yolanda. Oh, here, you can tell her personally." Yolanda was bringing iced coffee.

When we had finished dessert, Veronica and Sylvia wrapped up their business in her office, while I strolled out to the dock. The scene was truly idyllic. I sat on a chair by the water and almost fell asleep, so gentle and hypnotic was the lapping of the waves on the shore. When I got up and returned to the patio, I looked up for some reason. Perhaps it was movement, like the flutter of a bird's wing catching the eye. I was sure I saw Marco, standing at an upstairs window, looking down at me. Then, just as quickly as I saw him, he vanished.

60.

AFTER VERONICA AND SIMON left, Sylvia had gone directly to the workroom to talk to the women and devise a plan for completing the orders and sharing the workload. Veronica Masters's order was for ten different outfits in three sizes. Plus, Sylvia's friend in Granada would get an order for her jewellery. She was so caught up in her business that she hadn't noticed Marco's absence. It wasn't until the end of the day, when Yolanda was serving dinner and Marco didn't appear, that she went up to his room. She found him curled, foetus-like in the centre of the bed, trembling. She lay at his back and held him. His shirt was damp.

"How is your migraine?" she asked, speaking softly near his ear.

"Horrible. It has my head in its clutches and won't let go."

"Is there anything I can do? Should I call a doctor?"

"No. Nothing. I have to ride it out. Just leave me, please."

She hugged him, stood up, and went back downstairs.

Marco's mind raced. That gringo artist lived in his house; he'd obviously inherited Don Verde. But they didn't know Marco was from there, probably thought he was Nicaraguan. Don Verde, for Christ's sake! What was that bird saying? It wouldn't have stopped talking just because his owner had left. Don Verde had a broad repertoire of speech, as Marco recalled. It assaulted his mind in a sick, devious litany: "*muy lejos*" and "*mucho dinero*" *and* "*no me pegues*" were some of his favourites. Maybe the gringo didn't understand much Spanish. How could he tell Sylvia of this strange coincidence? He rolled over and continued to hug his knees. His head was pounding, but it wasn't a migraine.

Sylvia gave him his space that night and slept in her own room. When she got up the next morning and knocked on his door, there was no answer. She opened the door and found the bed rumpled, empty and cold to the touch. He wasn't on the balcony, and when she went downstairs, she saw that his car was not in the driveway.

61.

ANTONIO'S UNCLE had a boat and motor, and surprisingly, they found some gasoline and oil in the shed. The place was well-tended, but that was to be expected; Tío Juan José was meticulous. He would be frustrated as a convalescent, dependent on his daughter.

The property was midway between El Rama and Bluefields on the Rio Escondido. The river was almost ninety kilometres long from its source to the Caribbean Sea. Bluefields was the oldest coastal city in Nicaragua, dating back to 1602. Nearby was the Mosquito Coast. The area had been—and still was—a hiding place for pirates.

"How fitting that we come to a place like this. A safe haven for pirates," Nick said, leaning back at the prow of the boat. They were meandering along the slow-moving river. Crocodiles, eyes closed, lazed on the shoreline, sated. Nick kept his hands out of the water anyway. Sandpipers sprinted along the sand as if trying to keep up with the boat. In a nearby field, snowy egrets foraged in the wake of the grazing Brahman cattle. The air hummed with cicadas and bees at perfect pitch.

"The motor works well," Antonio reported. "Suppose I shouldn't have expected less from Tío."

"How far do you think it is to Bluefields?" Nick asked.

"I'd say thirty or forty kilometres. We couldn't do it in a day in this runabout, and I wouldn't risk taking it. If the motor breaks down, and we don't have a backup, we're screwed."

When pirates sought seclusion in and around Bluefields, it had often led them into the welcoming arms of the local women, tantalized by exciting tales of plundering. And so it would happen that those shady characters bred broods with the locals. The pirates may have sailed on for more lucrative waters, but their spawn remained, carrying on the family tradition of wheeling and dealing items with questionable provenance, embroidering dramatic stories, parroting others they'd heard. Nick and Antonio banked on the hope that the marketplace would still be active and alive with buyers and merchants of whatever stripe.

"I'll call Hector and get him to come up, so he can fly us out to Bluefields. Stay for a few days. Do some fishing. Shoot some crocs."

They packed their gear, plus one bag of raw jewels and gold jewellery. They'd book into a place for a couple of days, and, as Nick suggested, "suss out the 'hood."

Before he left, Tío Juan José had made sure that his house and buildings were secure. Likewise, when Antonio and Nick left for a few days, they locked all the windows and doors and secured their secret hiding places. They had their gear down at the dock to load when Hector arrived.

62.

IT WAS MID-JANUARY. Veronica had gone back to New York. Trying to get used to being alone again, I rattled around in the house and walked the beach for days on end. I had to appease myself with the knowledge that she'd be back in February for the exhibition at the hotel. I finally settled down and started to paint again. I had managed to complete two pieces while Veronica had been here over Christmas, and I still had two to finish in the next couple of weeks. I was painting on canvas now, had a local carpenter cut and assemble my stretchers, so I didn't have to worry about framing.

I had also agreed to receive the clothing order from Sylvia in Granada. I awaited instructions but knew I would probably have to go to the airport in Liberia. I think she said that she would transport the goods to Managua and put them on a flight from the airport there. Sounded costly to me, but that was not my problem.

Veronica babbled excitedly on our way back from Sylvia and Marco's place in Laguna de Apoyo. I had listened and nodded, trying to share her level of enthusiasm. But the image of Marco at the upstairs window kept reappearing in my mind's eye. Veronica had dismissed my suspicions, siding with the state of a person inflicted with a migraine.

"It's crippling. Those were your words, Simon. I got migraines when I was a teenager. I had to stay in the house with the blinds drawn. The pain was debilitating," she had said.

If that was the case, then why was he standing at the window? I wondered. He had seemed so agitated when he looked at my work. Don Verde, in particular, seemed to bother him. Parrot phobia? Bad childhood memories? Or maybe it really had been a bad migraine. Maybe something we'd eaten at lunch had triggered an allergic reaction.

63.

MARCO PAID A MAN to take him to Antonio's house on the island. He was sure they wouldn't be there. Didn't matter anyway. When he got in the boat, he closed his eyes and let the wind wash over his face. When they neared the island, the house was barely visible in the darkness.

"Thanks, man. Would you wait here while I go up? Shine your light on me until the sensor lights kick in and you're sure I can get in." Marco climbed out and went up the walk. A few metres up the path, the lights came on, and that portion of the island was illuminated.

"Thanks again." Marco waved and his buddy waved back, then gunned the engine and disappeared back down the channel. He went into the house and turned on the lights. It was obvious Antonio and Nick hadn't been there in a while. In the refrigerator, a swollen carton of milk had curdled and smelled vile. On the counter, a package of tortillas had curled out of their open plastic wrapper, so stale they were crisp. And rotting papaya and mangoes had turned into mush at the bottom of the crisper. He dumped the milk in the sink and rinsed it away, then took the fruit outside and put it on a bench under the Ceiba tree for the birds and iguanas. Beer didn't sour or go bad, and there was a good stock of it. He uncapped a Toña.

He wished he could talk to Tío Vincente. His uncle was experienced and knew the law better than he did. If Sylvia continued her business with the gringa, she would undoubtedly visit her some time. Maybe even ask him to go with her. He couldn't go back without risking a lengthy prison sentence if he was caught, and he couldn't seem to control his emotions. He had almost passed out when he'd seen Don Verde in one of the paintings on the website. If he couldn't control himself, his peculiar behaviour would be noticeable and, ultimately, suspicious. Several scenarios spooled out in his mind as he stared at the reflection of himself in the darkened window. He had to make some decisions. Sylvia needed to know the truth if she was going to marry him. And if he told her the entire story, would she keep his secret, or did he even *want t*o keep it? He needed to talk to someone. He went to bed. The faint hum of the refrigerator was the only sound in the house, yet the noise that reverberated in Marco's head kept him awake until dawn.

"Hello?" That response alone made him feel better before any other words were spoken.

"Hello Tío, this is Marco. How are you?"

"Not bad for an old fellow. How about you?" And with that question, Marco told his uncle about the woman in his life and the business dealings she had and where her customer and her artist friend lived in Costa Rica. That he was worried.

"How well were you known, and what kind of a profile did you have while you lived at Tamarindo? How long did you live there?"

"We'd only just moved there, maybe six months before, from San José. I wasn't around much, and Isabella kept to herself. Still, there are lots of nosy people around."

"You'll be travelling in other circles this time, Marco: the art world. Maybe you can avoid going near the old place."

"I don't see how that can be, especially if Sylvia wants to deliver the order personally, or be there for the show at the hotel."

"Then plan to meet them at the hotel. Book in well in advance. What hotel is it?" Vincente knew about all the coastal development and often the owners as well.

"That boutique hotel, Cala Luna."

"Victor Ramirez owns that place. Steep rates. Very exclusive. Drive there and stay put. Relax with your lady for a couple of days. She'd probably like that if she's been working so hard."

"Sounds so easy when you talk about it, Tío, but the whole thing, the coincidence of meeting those people, has been making me crazy."

"*Claro, mi hijo*. Nothing is coincidence. It's all part of the Great Plan."

"I hope you're right, Tío. It's been so peaceful until now, and even now, it's quiet, except for the noise in my head."

"That's why I pray, Marco." He cleared his throat before he continued. "And it has paid off, Marco. Sonia has come to me. She forgives me. I am so relieved."

When Marco went to bed that night, Isabella appeared at the foot of his bed. She had someone very familiar with her. That person was a well-dressed man with a long elegant moustache and styled hair that had faint streaks of blond in it, which was highlighted by the aura that surrounded them. The man looked very much like himself. Marco. Isabella smiled, appearing satisfied. Once again, he knew what he had to do.

64.

THEY FOUND A VILLA overlooking the harbour. Hector was happy to hang around for a few days. His time in the air had been almost double what pilots normally fly. After he'd brought the boys to the house on the river, he flew back to Granada to collect a couple of businessmen and fly them to Managua. He catnapped while he waited four hours for them to have lunch and complete their meeting; then, he returned them to Granada. He'd brought his fishing rod on this haul and planned to make good use of it.

Nick and Antonio sniffed around town while Hector fished. They found a bar down by the waterfront. They'd been told about a gringo named Gerry who lived in Bluefields, probably progeny of pirate ancestors. They found him, a salty dog who had so many tattoos he really didn't need to wear clothes, not that he wore many anyway. With little more than a thong tied around his crotch, his giant belly spilled over it to render his privates invisible. He wore a patch over one eye and a red bandana tied around his shaved—and tattooed—head. The only adornments he exhibited were his ruby pinky ring, so refined a setting for such a rough man, and a thick gold chain that hung below several chins of fat. Oh yes, Antonio noted a gold ring in his earlobe.

They had a beer at a table on their own, and when a couple of men who'd been sitting with Gerry left, Nick went over and slid into one of the chairs. They chatted. Nick returned and sat down. "Gerry wants to meet with us at his place tonight at six. Lives further up the cliff, almost above us."

Perhaps Gerry dressed for dinner. He greeted them in a caftan and bare feet, cigar in his mouth, still adorned with the requisite pieces of jewellery.

"Come in, gentlemen, come in. Welcome to Bluefields." They walked into an enormous open space that looked out onto the Caribbean. It had been designed like the prow of a ship; a great portion of the structure was cantilevered out over the ocean, giving the illusion that it was on the water. A long solid piece of gleaming mahogany set on legs served beautifully as a table, and they joined him at it in captain's chairs.

"Care for a drink?"

"No thanks, Gerry. I'll wait until after we've done business."

"Fair enough. But I hope you don't mind if I do." He waddled over to the refrigerator and took out ice, olives, and vodka. He mixed himself a dirty martini and returned to the table. "Nick tells me that you have some spoils from a treasure chest. Do a little diving, do you, Tony?"

"A bit," Antonio said and smiled. "We got lucky this time." He put a briefcase on the table and started unpacking the diamonds, emeralds, rubies, and sapphires. Some of the gemstones were loose, others set in yellow gold or platinum. Gerry whisked out his loupe and set it in against the fat around his eyes. It held. His breathing was laboured. Perspiration coated his face, and his caftan was probably absorbing what couldn't be seen. Gerry continued to grunt and sigh and burp. Antonio hoped he didn't expire before they made the deal.

"Fine specimens, lads. And you're in luck, I have a buyer coming in early next week. He'll love these gems." He started separating them into groups.

"I'll give you ten grand for the rubies and sapphires, thirty for the diamonds, and twenty for the emeralds. That's sixty grand in total."

"Hmmm," Nick said, rubbing the stubble on his chin. "We

were thinking more like eighty, Gerry."

"You're right, Nick. The total value for the works of it will get me about eighty grand, but my cut is twenty."

Nick looked at Antonio with a forlorn expression.

"What do you say, bro? Should we try elsewhere?"

"I'm the best there is on this coast before you get to San Andrés," Gerry said.

Nick and Antonio shrugged in unison.

"Then I guess we'll take it, Gerry," Nick said. "But I know you're going make more than twenty on it."

They'd accepted a couple of bottles of beer from Gerry when he made his second martini. They agreed later that they hadn't trusted him completely and didn't want to accept any mixed drinks from him. He couldn't do anything to a couple of beers he'd uncapped in front of them. They hadn't stayed long, and when they got back to the villa they hugged like long-lost brothers.

"I had no fucking idea what it was worth, man," Nick said. He laughed and handed Antonio a bottle of beer from the bar fridge. "Forgot to tell you that I told him we were divers and had found some buried treasure. Don't know if he bought it or not. I'm sure he hears all kinds of explanations for why people show up on his doorstep wanting to sell shit."

After they stashed the money, they sat on the porch basking in their victory like sated iguanas. They were both looking out at the emerald sea, daydreaming.

"You ever been married, Tony?" Nick asked.

"No, I haven't." Antonio continued gazing at the water. "I came close. Was engaged, but my *novia* was killed in a car accident."

"Jeez, man. Sorry to hear that."

"That's okay. It was years ago. What about yourself?"

"Oh yeah. I married my high-school sweetheart." Nick chugged his beer and went for another. "But she got tired of waiting for me while I was in the service, I guess. My best friend retired early because of a back injury, and she's with him now."

"Tough luck," Antonio said. "Don't think I could handle that."

"I couldn't either. That's why I'm here."

Hector arrived with a creel full of three hefty grouper, packed in ice, gutted, and cleaned. He stowed them in the refrigerator, grabbed a beer, and flopped next to Antonio on the sofa. His round face beamed like a Buddha.

"Good day, Hector?" Antonio asked.

"Excellent, Tonio. Good fishing. Good people."

"Oh yeah? What kind of good people?" Nick asked from his roost in a hammock across from them.

"Met an old Rasta-like dude named Consolación. Such a deep voice. Truly a gentleman. Said he was the great-great grandson of a slave who'd served for William Walker in Granada. Poor Consolación has a rough life, trying to feed his family. I gave him a couple of the fish I caught." Once again, the name conjured up the dream Nick had had, months ago. A coincidence, no doubt, but the name was unusual. He'd looked it up in his Spanish-English dictionary. It meant the same in English: "to offer comfort."

"I'd like to meet him, Hector," said Nick. "Are you going fishing tomorrow?"

"Sure, if you guys have no other plans."

The next morning, after a hearty breakfast of fish, eggs, beans, and tortillas, they all went to the docks where Hector had fished the previous day. The old man was already there, pole in the water, concentrating on the ebb and flow. Hector introduced his friends to him.

"Pleased to meet you, Consolación," Nick said, still visibly shaken by the name, gripping the old man's hand a little too tight. When he released his hand, Consolación rubbed his gnarled knuckles.

"Arthritis in my paws. You've got quite a grip there, Nick."

His voice was deep and syrupy and familiar. He winked at Nick like they shared a secret.

"How many you got in your family, Consolación?" Nick asked.

"Seventeen," the old man replied, grinning with far fewer teeth than he had children.

"Well, we would like you and your family to be our guests at dinner tonight," Nick said. He grinned at Antonio before he continued. "Consolación, we are going to have an evening that I hope you and your family will enjoy and remember for a long time."

Later that day, with help from the resort, they arranged picnic tables—with tablecloths, dishes, and cutlery—for a feast that Hector and Nick prepared of chicken, crabs, and steak. Antonio went to find refreshments, vegetables, and sweets.

Just before sunset, a ragtag group spaced according to size and age, like the keys on a marimba, approached the villa. Consolación brought up the rear with his wife on his arm. As they approached, Nick moved closer to Antonio.

"These kids move with such respectful grace," he told Antonio. "Gringo kids would be running and screaming and carrying on." As they filed over to them, each child first shook Nick then Antonio's hand. A couple of the little girls curtsied and giggled. They were shy and probably didn't really know why they were there, except at the bidding of their father. Two beautiful young women arrived next. Identical twins. Nick and Antonio smiled at them and shook their hands. Their names were Rocío, which meant "morning dew," and Estrella, which meant "star." When Consolación arrived, Nick hugged him like a long-lost relative. He turned with the old man and faced his family. As Nick spoke, Antonio translated for him.

"Welcome everyone. Please have a seat. Make yourselves at home. Thanks be to God that we are all here together. Let's eat." Platters of steaming crabs, barbecued steak, chicken, rice, and vegetables covered the tables and with Nick's brief, almost incidental grace, they crossed themselves and started to fill their plates. It appeared they were all hungry and little was said while they all savoured the feast. Pitchers of iced juices were set on the table, and when everyone's glasses were filled, Nick rose from the table.

"We have invited you here this evening to honour you and to remember and honour your ancestors, who lived at the mercy of the tyrant, William Walker. He was merciless in his quest for power, and many people suffered. Because I am an American citizen, I feel responsible for his wrongdoing. So, on behalf of the United States of America, I want to say that I am truly sorry for his mistakes." Nick stood beside Consolación and put his hands on his shoulders. "It was wrong that this man enslaved your ancestors. I do not agree with what he did or what he thought. But words are not enough." He looked across at Antonio before he continued. "We would like to give you some money so that your children can go to school. We will provide enough for you to buy uniforms and all the books and supplies that the children will need to attend until they graduate. It is a small token, but it is given in respect."

Before Consolación and his family left that night, Nick quietly handed him a fat envelope filled with American bills totalling ten thousand dollars. The old man didn't count it but could tell it was more money than he'd earned in his life. He swiped at the tears that welled in his eyes. He hugged Nick.

"*Muchisima gracias, hijo. Que Dios los bendiga.*" Thank you very much, son. God bless you.

65.

WHEN MARCO FINISHED his call to Tío Vincente, he called Sylvia. Yolanda answered. Sylvia was out rowing. She would get her to call. He left the landline number on the island. He made some more coffee and waited. She called in less than twenty minutes.

"Marco, how are you?"

"I'm better now, thanks. How are you?"

"I'm fine, but I've been worried about you and where you'd gone. You're on the island?"

"Yes. Antonio and Nick aren't here. Don't know where they are. I've missed you, Sylvia. But please understand that I needed to be alone, to sort through some stuff."

"And? Have you done that?"

"I hope so. I'll be back later this afternoon. Since I don't have a boat, I'm at the mercy of the guys who have them. They might be out on tours. I'll get there as soon as I can."

"Is everything alright, Marco?"

"Between us? Everything is superb. I love you madly. And I think I've sorted the other stuff out, too. We'll talk when I get home."

He called a water taxi, and it came fifteen minutes later. He got his car and parked near Claro Americas and walked to the cathedral. He knelt at the altar and prayed for guidance. He lit four candles and said four prayers. When he left the church, he went to a salon where he had his hair cut, styled, and bleached with blond streaks. Then, he left for Laguna de Apoyo. He opened the two front windows and let the cooling air refresh him. He rubbed the stubble above his lip, the start of a moustache he hoped would one day be as elegant as his uncle Vincente's. At the moment, though, it felt itchy like a crusty rash, but his hair and beard grew quickly, and hopefully the itch would soon subside.

Sylvia heard the SUV and ran out to meet him. She held him at arm's-length, examining his new look. They embraced and didn't say anything, but then both started at the same time. She deferred.

"I'm sorry I ran off without telling you. Very childish of me."

"Whatever. You're here now." They walked back to the house where the level of activity was feverish. Three sewing machines were running like gentle woodpeckers tapping out stitches. They peeked into the room and Marco greeted the women. They nodded and smiled, continued with their work. Marco and Sylvia continued through to the patio and sat down.

"So, Marco. What 'stuff' have you been sorting out?" She didn't sound aggressive, just curious, like any fiancée would be. He looked around, wondering if anyone was within earshot.

"It's a very long story. But the upshot is that Veronica and Simon must have bought my house when I left Costa Rica. They inherited Don Verde." He stalled when he saw her smiling. "What? What's so amusing?"

"I can't understand why seeing a painting of him would affect you so much."

"It isn't just that. Don Verde is very intelligent and he talks very well. He..." Marco stalled again. "I'm going to go and get some water." He tried to stand, but Sylvia put her hand on his shoulder, pressing him back into the chair.

"Sit. I'll get Yolanda to bring some." She trotted away, and in seconds had returned and sat with her hands clasped on the table. "Continue." He waited until Yolanda had left the pitcher of water and glasses.

He told her how he had trained and used Don Verde to deliver drugs to freighters moored offshore, and to return with the money from the sales. That he'd done it several times.

"So what's the big deal? That's over and done with."

"It's just that Don Verde spoke a lot and often repeated a number of phrases that were related to the work he was doing." He couldn't tell her what else the bird said, what he'd heard so many times.

"I wouldn't worry about it, Marco. Simon says the bird speaks English now, so maybe he's forgotten what you taught him." She stood and went over to him and rubbed his shoulders. "I've got to go back to work now, but we'll talk more—if you want—at dinner."

66.

I WAS OFF THE HOOK. This morning, I received an email from Sylvia in Laguna de Apoyo, telling me that I didn't need to drive to the airport. She and Marco would deliver the order personally to the hotel, well in advance of the opening. Apparently, Marco was taking her on a holiday after she and the other women completed the order. I was relieved because I was still not finished painting.

I was working on a triptych of the leatherback turtles. It had been easy to monitor the nest each day, and sure enough, one evening at the end of January, I witnessed the sand ripple with subterranean activity. Before too long, tiny little hatchlings struggled to the surface and plowed their little flippers through the sand to the ocean. I called Veronica that night to announce the hatch. Her excitement rippled over the phone line. I'd decided to keep quiet about my triptych.

The first panel depicted the turtle arriving on shore, like a surfer, selecting the final wave that would thrust her onto the sand. The second panel combined the motion of her excavating flippers as well as laying eggs. I was close to finishing the third, which was their post-hatch exodus. I didn't want to show it or photograph it until I'd completed the third, to tell the entire story. Maria was the only person to see them, and that was just in passing. They were different from Don Verde's portraits, more dramatic. I hoped I had captured the struggle of these critically endangered creatures. Despite this struggle, I was reassured to know that the shoreline right in front of my house was protected. I felt like a proud parent. I couldn't remember the percentage of the little gaffers that ultimately made it to maturity, but it was few. I did remember that Veronica had said their numbers had fallen to a fraction of what once existed and I hoped my homage to them would perhaps reach an audience that would be sensitive to their fragility on the planet.

I finished the final panel three days before Veronica would arrive in Liberia and spent the rest of the afternoon organizing my canvases. I wrote a manifest for Veronica and Cala Luna, then opened a beer and chilled out with Don Verde on the veranda. Maria had left for the day. She and Don Verde must have been singing a song that Maria taught him while she was staying here, and he sang it to me.

67.

AT DAYBREAK, Sylvia and Marco drove down from Laguna de Apoyo to San Jorge, north of Rivas. They went to Las Hamacas, the same hotel where he and Antonio had stayed when he did the Ometepe trip. When they arrived, it was still mid-morning and the rooms weren't ready, so they checked their bags and went out to the terrace restaurant and had breakfast. While they waited to be served, Marco opened his cellphone, found a name, and pressed the call button.

"Hi Diego, this is Marco. Yes, my fiancée and I are in San Jorge. We're heading down to Costa Rica for a holiday, and I don't have insurance coverage for the SUV outside of Nicaragua. Wondered if you could do me a favour tomorrow morning. I'd be happy to pay you. No, seriously. Come to Las Hamacas in a taxi, then drive us in the SUV to the border, where we'll walk across. You come back here and put the car in a secure parking lot, and I'll call you when we're ready to return. Then you come to the border to get us. Appreciate it. Thanks, Diego. See you tomorrow morning about nine." He shut the phone and winked at Sylvia.

Diego arrived just after nine the following morning and within less than an hour they were at Peñas Blancas Customs and Immigration. Marco shook hands with Diego, and in the gesture, pressed fifty dollars into his hand and said he'd call him. He hoisted his bag over his shoulder and pulled one of Sylvia's. She had packed two large suitcases on wheels; Veronica's order and jewellery were in them, with room to spare for Sylvia's outfits and toiletries. They were nearing Costa Rican Immigration.

"So, do you want me to go order some soft drinks and sandwiches while you go and deal with Customs?" he asked.

"You can do that, but I am going to say that the contents are mine and gifts for my family. If they examine them really closely, they might become suspicious of the three sizes of each outfit, and if they do, well, I'll just pay the duty."

"That's my little criminal talking."

A tour bus had entered just before them, and by the time they queued and waited their turns, their passports were summarily stamped by a tired clerk, ready for his break. They walked through the doors of that building outside of which there was another holding area. They hoisted their bags onto a conveyor belt that moved each bag into an X-ray scanning device. And just as easy as claiming the luggage at the other end of the machine, they were in Costa Rica.

"Welcome to my country, *mi amor*." He kissed her, then hoisted his bag over his shoulder and grabbed the handle of one of her suitcases.

When they got out past the government buildings and Duty Free, Marco flagged a taxi to take them to a car rental agency. In a half-hour, they were inside a similar though stripped-down version of Marco's SUV heading south.

Sylvia was captivated by the landscape, and when she rolled down the windows, the salty air blew her hair back, and she giggled like a little girl. She smiled widely at Marco as he reached out an arm to caress her face. It made his heart stop to see her so happy.

When they entered the grounds of Cala Luna, she gasped. "Is this the place? It's incredible. This is where the show will be?"

"Yes, this is the place and I agree, it is incredible. And yes, this is where the show will be." Marco laughed and put his hand on hers. "I love you so much."

When they pulled in the circular drive, a man in a T-shirt with "Cala Luna" printed across the pocket greeted them and said he would park their car, and that his partner would be out to get the luggage. He directed them through the doors to reception.

The villa Marco selected had a spacious pool set in a patio and garden, a large Jacuzzi bathtub, and a completely stocked and outfitted kitchen. The king-sized bed looked diminutive in the bedroom that extended to garden doors and a patio where offshore breezes clattered melodically through a bamboo hedge. Sylvia walked into his outstretched arms.

"We're actually on a holiday, my darling," he told her. "Perhaps this is a rehearsal for our *luna de miel*."

They fell onto the pillowy bed and snuggled until they both fell asleep. The sun was setting when Sylvia roused. She rummaged in the refrigerator and found paté, cheese, and olives. She put a plate together with some crackers, and after she had opened a bottle of wine, she slid open the door to the patio and left Marco to sleep. She had only nibbled a couple of olives and sipped her wine when he emerged, stretching. She poured a glass for him. He kissed her on the cheek and sat down at the table.

"I slept so deeply. Must have been tired from the trip. Did you sleep?"

"Oh yes. I've only been up a short while. It's so relaxing here."

The next morning, after breakfast, they walked along the beach, paddled in the shallows, and relaxed under a *palapa* on chaise lounges. Sylvia had new issues of *Vogue* and *Elle* and was pouring over them, turning corners down on pages of fashions she liked. Marco sat upright and looked out at the ocean, sipping a beer, remembering when he used to ride the waves here. A short distance down the beach, a family was setting up beneath another *palapa*. Two men hovered in the background, obviously not prepared for the beach in their black pants and T-shirts that stretched taut over their muscled biceps.

Bodyguards? To Marco's eyes, the family wasn't Tico. Perhaps Colombian or Mexican, Marco thought. Either way, they were rich. This was apparent by the presence of a nanny who took care of two small children, and from all the gold jewellery. Hefty gold chains hung around the man's neck, and earrings and bangles dripped from his wife's earlobes and arms. The third child, their first-born, was a teenage boy with attitude, visible in his body language. He was probably wishing he were somewhere else, maybe missing a girlfriend who might be the recipient of his current texts. Marco leaned back and thought about being a father. He reached over and caressed Sylvia's leg. She looked at him and smiled, continued reading.

When he looked again, the tableau down the beach had changed. The mother was lying flat on her back on the lounge, the father was pacing the beach, waving his arms back and forth, perhaps exercising, his gold jewellery glittering in the sunlight. The children were with the nanny, making a sand-castle in the damp sand at the edge of the outgoing tide. The kid? The kid was out of the picture. Marco looked out over the water and saw arms stroking through the water, the only person swimming. Marco had come here to surf years ago before Cala Luna existed and knew that the undertow was powerful; even the best on a surfboard could take a tumble and be sucked down. He hadn't taken his eyes off the water, but now he couldn't see the kid at all. He jumped up suddenly and ran to the beach, plowing into the water. The kid was fighting, struggling, probably very scared. As Marco got close enough, and the kid bobbed up, he yelled and signalled him to move sideways. Swimming out at a forty-five-degree angle, you could get out of the arc of the undertow. He didn't think the kid heard or understood. Marco continued swimming in his direction, and when he bobbed up the next time, he grabbed one of the kid's arms and started propelling him sideways. The boy was weak, and when he was able to manoeuver him to calmer water, he rolled him on his back, put his arm around the boy's neck and clawed, sideways through the water, back to shore. He then lifted the boy and slung him over his shoulder like a wet bag of rice and slogged up the beach.

Marco didn't know how long he'd been gone, but onshore the tableau had changed once again, Sylvia had joined the mother and father at the water's edge. Only the little ones seemed unconcerned and continued their castle construction. The mother was wringing her hands and crying. The father paced on the spot. The nanny flitted like an agitated wren between the children and her employers. Sylvia looked concerned.

When Marco laid the kid down on the sand and gave him CPR, the family encircled him. "He swallowed a lot of water," Marco explained between breaths, pressing gently on the boy's rib cage. After a few attempts, the boy started to cough; he sputtered and spewed water and bile into the sand.

"*Gracias a Dios. Lo salvaste, mi hijo*." The mother was effusive, trying to speak through her tears, now tears of joy. Marco couldn't tell for sure, but her accent sounded Mexican. She spoke quietly to her husband who nodded. She knelt on the sand and brushed the hair back from her boy's face. He was somewhat subdued in comparison to his former surly posture.

The father came forward and extended his hand. "My name is Felipe. Felipe Montoya," he said, then looked down. "My wife, Marta, and the boy you saved is my son, Alfonso."

"My name is Marco Alvarez Soto, and this is my fiancée, Sylvia."

"You are very brave to have risked your life for a stranger."

"Thank you. I used to surf when I was younger, and I know how dangerous the waters are around here. I got concerned when I saw Alfonso near what we used to call the Danger Zone."

"I can't thank you enough, Marco. As a small token of our appreciation would you be our guests at dinner tonight?"

Marco looked at Sylvia who smiled and then back at Felipe. "We would be honoured."

"I think you have it reversed, Marco. *We* would be honoured.

See you at seven in the dining room." He shook Marco's hand again and helped Alfonso, who limped back to their *palapa*.

The dining room was next to one of the pools. The area was lit with hurricane lamps and stronger diffused light from the covered dining area. Felipe and Marta were standing by the pool when Marco and Sylvia arrived.

"Good evening, Sylvia, Marco." Felipe bowed ever so slightly. He sparkled in his white cotton pants and loose collarless shirt, accessorized with his gold jewellery. Marta wore a sleeveless floor-length coral sheath and a complimentary lightweight pashmina. She'd changed the gold she'd been wearing earlier in the day for diamonds and coral. Felipe extended his arm in the direction of the partially covered dining room. "Shall we?"

Several couples sat at tables near the pool and in a corner of the covered dining room. It appeared that Felipe had made reservations and from the vacant tables in the immediate vicinity of their table, it seemed he had also asked for space around them, void of other diners. But gringos ate early and Ticos wouldn't arrive for another hour or more, so they had a natural privacy zone anyway. A bottle of champagne chilled in an ice bucket at one end of the table, flutes at the ready. When everyone had settled, Felipe motioned for the waiter who ceremoniously uncorked the champagne. He poured four glasses, and when he had returned the bottle to the ice bucket and disappeared, Felipe stood.

"We are gathered this evening to honour and give our most sincere thanks to Marco Alvarez Soto and his brave rescue of my son, Alfonso. We are indebted to you, Marco. Let us drink to Marco." Just then, a flashbulb went off. Then another. A reporter and photographer descended on the table.

"Señor Montoya. We heard about your son's rescue from the undertow. You are no doubt grateful that you haven't lost another child. Is this the man who saved your son? May we talk to you both?"

Felipe's face grew stormy. He lunged at them but was prevented from making contact when his bodyguards secured both photographer and reporter. He roared at his two men, and one of them took the photographer's camera, flung it hard on the terrazzo floor, and smashed it with his size fourteen boots.

"I apologize, Marco. They're parasitic pariahs, the paparazzi, all of them. I don't know how they got in here." He sat down and drank his champagne.

"Your apology is accepted, but I didn't know we were dining with celebrities."

"Believe me, you're not. They're hungry parasites, all of them. Maybe they saw us arrive in the marina and asked who we are. Kidnapping for ransom is a popular sport these days. Hence, the need for bodyguards, so that we avoid elimination." He took another sip. "We sailed down from Puerto Ángel in Oaxaca. My yacht is in the marina in Tamarindo, getting some work done on the engine. At sea, no one bothered us. I thought we could come to Cala Luna and relax, have some peace and quiet, but as you see, life intervened and set a series of actions in motion that brought the paparazzi. Now you know my story. Let us relax and eat."

A previously selected course of hot and cold shrimp appetizers had arrived and were being arranged in front of them. "Let us enjoy this fine food and good company." He summoned one of the waiters and told him to bring some Riesling. This time when their wine was poured, Felipe did not stand, and he spoke more quietly, but still effusively thanked Marco for his valiant rescue of Alfonso.

"You are more than welcome, Felipe," Marco said, growing uncomfortable with all the attention. "Why did you mention kidnapping and your need for bodyguards?"

"As you might have gathered, we live in Oaxaca, Mexico. When we're there," he said, looking at his wife. "We're taking the year off. We both needed a rest. Our daughter was kidnapped eighteen months ago. We paid the ransom, but still they killed her. We mourn her death still. My workers have operated my farm for years, so I've left it in their capable hands." Felipe sipped his wine, thoughtfully. "And you two. Tell us about yourselves."

Marco and Sylvia alluded to their work in the most general of terms. But when Sylvia spoke of the upcoming art exhibition and that her line of clothing was being featured, Marta perked up, excited to be next to someone who shared her passion for fashion. By the time coffee and liqueurs were served, Felipe promised them both a sailing trip, once the engine had been repaired and Sylvia had her exhibition.

68.

NOW THAT I WAS painting on canvas and each one was on a stretcher, I put the seats down in the back of the car and stacked the paintings, supported between our bags. I managed to hide the triptych before Veronica arrived two days ago. She was so excited and distracted that she hadn't bothered to count the pieces, anyway. I was glad I had finished painting and could give her all my attention. It was an impressive feat that she'd accomplished with some serendipitous opportunities. Eric Connors, her working partner, had turned out to be a crackerjack marketer. In the brief month he'd been involved at the Lasting Image Gallery, sales had increased ten percent over the last year's January sales. That was saying a lot.

She had been in touch with Victor Ramirez at the Cala Luna, discussing space to hang my paintings. Victor had suggested the walls of the grand foyer at reception, along the wall of the broad staircase, and the mezzanine leading to the suites on the second floor. There were directional halogen lights, and he had more should we need them. He also had acquired some handsome wrought-iron racks to display Sylvia's pieces. He'd announced the exhibition on Cala Luna's website weeks in advance of the show, and he told us that he had posters up in the area. Veronica had provided him with photos of my paintings and Sylvia's modelled clothes and jewellery to use in his layouts. She'd contacted Sylvia, and they had both agreed on which of Sylvia's outfits to wear at the opening.

Every time she finished a telephone conversation, she beamed.

We left my house after lunch on Wednesday and were unloading the car less than an hour later at Playa Langosta. Sylvia and Marco were already there. Marco's hair looked different—he'd streaked it, and he was sporting a handsome moustache that looked good on him, almost elegant. They helped us unload and carry the paintings into reception. I gave Veronica and Victor copies of my manifest, and as I brought each one in, I named the pieces so they could tick them off as received. When we got to *Perilous Journey*, the triptych, Veronica squealed like someone had pinched her.

"The leatherbacks! You painted them. You didn't tell me. They're wonderful." She hugged me and looked down at the canvases. "What a wonderful tribute to these amazing creatures."

We had coffee and then started to hang the show. *Perilous Journey* would hang along the expansive staircase and could easily be viewed from the mezzanine as well as the foyer. Sylvia's pieces were hanging on racks in Victor's office, ready to be wheeled out and taken up in the elevator to the mezzanine for the opening on Friday.

"We seem to be attracting a lot of attention," Veronica said.

I looked around to see several people standing at the entrance. She climbed onto a stepladder and adjusted one of the canvases. "Is that straight now?"

Marco and Sylvia were among the people standing near the entrance. They were speaking to a couple they appeared to be familiar with. Marco gestured for them to come inside.

"Felipe and Marta Montoya, I'd like you to meet artist, Simon Patrick, and his partner, Veronica Masters. Veronica has a gallery in New York and wants to spend more time here in Costa Rica with Simon. This exhibition will give her some indication if it would be profitable to open a gallery here."

"If my wife's enthusiasm for Sylvia's clothing is any indication, I am confident you will have a paying proposition." Felipe smiled. "But we don't want to interrupt your preparations, so if you'll excuse us, we are going for a swim. Very good to meet you both. Good luck hanging the show."

69.

ANTONIO AND NICK paid Hector for his holiday—on the condition that he was at their beck and call. From Bluefields, they got him to fly to Little Corn Island for a few days, where he could fish, and Antonio and Nick could snorkel around the reefs. When they'd had their feast with Consolación and his family back in Bluefields, the old man had told them that many of his people had fled to Little Corn Island following the conflagration of Granada. They hoped to meet some more descendants of the slaves who'd worked under William Walker's reign and share their spoils with them as well. Hector's interest in fishing always had social rewards, and often he returned with more stories than fish. On Little Corn Island, he brought back a little of both. The fish was Kingfish mackerel and the stories were historical family lore.

"Luís and Cristian, two brothers, invited me back to their place, a little shack on stilts just a little ways from the water," Hector told them. He was lying in one of the hammocks, sipping a beer. "We fried some clams that we'd dug in a beautiful, clean estuary with a sandy bottom. Dug them out with our bare feet, grasped the clams with our toes, and threw them into the boat. Bought some beer, smoked some weed, and filled our bellies with clams. They even offered me a hammock like this one, and we all kicked back for an hour in the heat of the day. Then, they took me to another spot where we caught a mess of fish. We drank some more beer, and they told me stories about their ancestors, some who'd floated over here on rafts. Said they'd rather be eaten by sharks than go back. Of course, William Walker had left by then, but the two-year nightmare had been etched, branded, maybe, into their hearts."

Once again, Nick and Antonio accompanied Hector to meet with his new buddies, and hung out at their shack for a while before they went fishing. Nick looked around at their meagre holdings. He watched as they rowed out from shore. He and Antonio went to a new cove to snorkel, and after having some lunch in town, Nick suggested they go back to a marina they'd passed on their way in and look at outboard motors.

"Those guys could sure use one. Make life a lot easier for them." They went back to the marina and bought the best fifty-horsepower motor, a full tank of gas plus a full jerry can, life preservers, a cooler that they later filled with ice and beer, and had it delivered to the dock before the boys returned.

The next day, Hector flew them to the airport in San Andrés, and returned to Little Corn Island, to fish and await word of his next assignment. Flying so low, so close to the water, they'd been able to see schools of colourful fish and pink coral that rose like mountain ranges beneath the water. After they'd checked into the hotel Nick's friends had suggested, they went to the bar. Junior and Buddy, Nick's friends, were there to meet them. Antonio was pretty sure those weren't their real names.

Junior and Buddy were ex-Marines, too. They'd done their share of smuggling drugs during their tours of duty, and now, they were into buying and selling precious gems. San Andrés was a free port, governed by Colombia. The main streets teemed with merchants marketing raw emeralds or finished emerald designs set in gold. They could buy gems or pieces of jewellery here, take them to the U.S., and double their money after expenses.

They sat on lawn chairs beneath a makeshift awning at a woman's beachside kitchen and drank ice-cold beer from her cooler as they peeled the shrimp she'd boiled in broth. Then, they all piled in the boat and motored the short distance to a cove where the two men had rented a villa. They climbed out of the boat and walked up to the house where a cat slept in a rocking chair in the shade of the vine-covered veranda. Nick and Antonio sat and waited while the guys tied up the boat. The cat jumped onto Nick's lap and rubbed her head against his chest.

"Just throw her off if she bothers you," Buddy said. "She's sort of adopted us." He unlocked the front door. "Want to come in or sit out there? It ain't air-conditioned, but we got lots of fans." They opted to stay outside.

Buddy brought out his jeweller's loupe, scales, calipers, and a piece of black velvet. Junior sprawled in a hammock and watched the proceedings. They sat around the glass-covered patio table, Buddy eyeing the jewellery and gems as Nick pulled them out, one by one. Like obese Gerry had in Bluefields, Buddy started making little piles of the pieces, sorting them by size, quality, and appearance. When he'd looked at the final ring in Nick's bag, he leaned back in his chair and stroked his chin as if he had a beard. His eyes flashed and flickered as his mind flipped numbers like a calculator.

"I'll take it off your hands for thirty grand."

"Off our hands?" Nick repeated derisively. "I was thinking about twice that, Buddy."

"Not a chance, Nick."

"Fifty, then."

Buddy looked at Nick like a small child who had just asked for the keys to his car. He looked out over the water before he spoke. "Forty. Period. End of story."

Nick stood up and paced back and forth on the veranda. He lit a cigarette and hauled on it. He looked at Antonio who grimaced and shrugged his shoulders. He walked back to the table and sat down. "Okay. Forty grand."

Buddy started gathering up the jewellery, but Nick put his

hands over Buddy's. "Uh-uh. Let's see the money first. We'll watch this while you get it. Junior is here to keep an eye on us, and where would we go anyway? We're on an island, remember."

Buddy groaned and rolled his eyes. He loped into the house, and a few minutes later returned with a canvas night deposit bag and handed it to Nick, who unzipped the bag and counted the money. "Good stuff. We're good to go, mate. You know the number for a taxi?" He stuffed the bag into his backpack and slung it over his shoulder while Buddy punched a number on his cellphone.

"Ready, Tony? Might as well walk out to the road and meet it. Thanks for your hospitality, Buddy, Junior. Night night, guys."

70.

ON FRIDAY AFTERNOON, Marco walked the beach while Sylvia and Veronica arranged the clothes on the mezzanine. He felt relaxed and stronger than he had when he first met Simon and Veronica at the fashion show. He'd behaved poorly, but feigning a migraine was all he'd been able to think to do. That shock was over, and now that he knew who they were, he was sure he could hold it together. However, if they continued socializing, he knew that Simon and Veronica would invite him and Sylvia to their home in Tamarindo. Maybe not this time, but sometime. He'd deal with that when it happened. He looked north, and in his mind's eye saw his shoreline, Simon's now, the dune grasses waving in the offshore winds. And then a figure appeared in his line of vision. Felipe was out walking, too. The two men continued to approach each other and finally met. They shook hands. Felipe patted Marco's shoulder in what Marco interpreted as enduring gratitude.

"We've been abandoned by our wives," he said. "I think Marta has joined Sylvia and Veronica in their preparations. We'll make the best of it, no?" Marco turned and started walking alongside Felipe. It was low tide, and the sand they walked on was firm, salty. Cool on their bare feet. "The show is going to be magnificent, don't you think?"

"Yes, Simon is a great artist, and Sylvia has a stunning line of clothing. I think it will go well together."

"I think Marta has made a few selections and will wear one

of them this evening. Three beautiful models should have no problem selling the clothes. And I have my eye on the *Perilous Journey.*"

"It's very evocative, isn't it? Are there leatherback turtles in your part of the Pacific?" Marco asked. He was thinking about the turtles he'd seen coming up on shore when he lived at Playa Tamarindo.

"I saw more when I was a child. Fewer now because of oil spills. Another species added to the critically endangered." Felipe reached down and picked up a piece of driftwood that had washed up on the shore. "How much extinction will we see in our lives, Marco?" Felipe tossed the stick, which flipped end over end before settling on the water. He continued, "We remember birds, lizards, and frogs we saw when we were young that our children have never seen in the flesh, only in textbooks or on the internet. I have seen leatherbacks in the sea, and watched as they came up at night to lay their eggs. I've watched them hatch, and make their way back into the ocean. And their journey *is* perilous, as Simon so aptly titled the triptych."

When they'd reached the path to Marco's villa, Marco extended his hand to Felipe. "If you will excuse me, Felipe, I'm going in for a nap and a shower. I'll see you in a couple of hours." The two men parted, and as Marco entered the suite, Isabella was there to greet him. She wiped perspiration that beaded his brow with fingers as light as feathers, and kissed him on the cheek.

71.

FELIPE CONTINUED WALKING along the beach, which had become peopled with swimmers and sunbathers since he'd started out earlier in the morning. A little girl with a broad-brimmed hat was playing with a bucket of sand by the water's edge. She looked so much like his daughter that he almost called out to her but quickly stopped himself. Alejandra wasn't with them. She would never be with them again. Only memories of her eight short years with them as a family would remain. And on this trip, he'd almost lost his son, were it not for Marco's quick response. He felt like a curse hung over him, watching and waiting until the right time to strike. His business prospered but the grief his family had suffered—was suffering—had become debilitating. Money or property could never replace Alejandra.

Felipe Montoya owned four hundred hectares of rich, fertile land in the mountains of Oaxaca—land he'd inherited when his father died more than twenty years ago. The land had passed through several generations, dating back to the eighteenth century when their ancestor Ferdinand Montoya arrived from Madrid. Family lore, passed down to each family member, romanticized their ancestor with stories about him falling in love with the daughter of a Zapotec chieftain. They married, and the land was a wedding gift. The Zapotec were on the land when coffee beans were first introduced to them from Veracruz, where it had arrived at about the same time as his ancestor. They started cultivating the plant. And when Ferdinand Montoya settled there, he continued to grow it, clearing more land, propagating more seedlings, until coffee covered the entire acreage. Today, descendants of those plants flourished on their mountainous land near the coast. Pineapple trees formed a natural fence along three sides of the expansive property beyond which was jungle, and to the west, the Pacific Ocean. It was rugged terrain beyond the plantation; the only roads were those that Montoya had built for his oxen to trudge with their wooden carts. Felipe had kept them groomed to provide a route for the trucks at harvest time, wide and long enough to accommodate his small Cessna, but beyond them, the jungle was thick, passage impossible. The plantation was visible only from the air.

And from the air, surveillance from some craft must have alerted one of the cartels cultivating opium, who sent one of their representatives to strike a deal with Felipe. One day, two muscular men drove onto the property in a Hummer the colour of gun metal. Felipe's watchman had led them to a shed where Felipe was watching one of his men roast coffee beans. The men were friendly, shaking hands with Felipe and complimenting him on his operation. He had just made some coffee to test and offered the men some. They'd gone outside and sat on chairs overlooking the plantation. The men had continued praising Felipe's land, told him that they had a "party" that was interested in it, and that this party could offer him more than his coffee plants could provide in income.

Felipe remembered smiling, chuckling, and telling them he wasn't interested in selling or leasing his property. They seemed to take the answer calmly enough. They finished their coffee, shook his hand, climbed back into their vehicle, and drove away. A week later, when he was out in one of the fields, he was surprised to see a helicopter hovering above him. It landed in a nearby gravelled area where his trucks loaded. A small, swarthy man climbed out of it carrying a briefcase, followed by one of the men from the previous visit. They approached Felipe who'd neared the parking lot where the chopper had landed. They both shook hands with him and spent a few moments praising the view. Then, the swarthy man opened his briefcase to reveal stacks of American bills bundled in elastic bands. He offered Felipe the money. Once again, Felipe said no. As he stared out at the ocean, Felipe winced when he recalled the man's parting words.

"I think you're making a mistake, Señor Montoya." He'd smiled and walked away. If Felipe had taken the money, would Alejandra still be alive?

She'd gone to school that day, but when his driver went for her in the afternoon, the children she had been with said she'd left with two men. Two men in a big grey vehicle. Before sunset, the phone rang at Felipe's house. Alejandra would be released if he paid them five hundred thousand U.S. dollars within twenty-four hours. He'd emptied his safe and come up with more than half. The next morning, he called his bank and arranged to extend his line of credit. The other children weren't aware that anything was wrong. However, Marta and Felipe spent a sleepless night, holding onto each other, trying to remain positive. He flew to Oaxaca City early the next morning to get the money. He returned home and had spent the next three hours pacing and trying to soothe Marta. In less than twenty-four hours, his beautiful wife looked so much older. Her hair hung limp over her stooped shoulders. Lines creased her sculptured face—a face that could transform, like a flower opening, when she smiled. He'd watched her kneeling at the altar of their family chapel, beeswax candles lit, sticks of Copal incense burning, its fragrance wafting, drifting on the breeze. But Marta couldn't hold the posture and collapsed on the rail, her shoulders heaving as she sobbed. It was time. He stepped up to the altar and put his hands on her trembling shoulders.

"I'm going now, Marta," he'd told her. "I'm going to get Alejandra."

He'd driven his ATV out to the parking area where the helicopter would land. It was about an hour before sunset. Iguanas scattered on the trail as he drove over their pathway. When he parked on the edge of the gravelled expanse, he stood looking towards the ocean, a barely visible but strong presence on the rich landscape around him. He heard the chopper before he saw the light beaming in, lowering slowly, noisily stirring up dust from the gravel. A wiry, little man climbed out of the chopper. Where was Alejandra? When the engine was turned off, the man approached Felipe. He smiled and extended his hand. Felipe ignored him.

"Where is my daughter?" he remembered hissing at the little man he towered over, the little cretin who wore cowboy boots with three-inch heels. Felipe didn't intimidate the man though.

"The money, first, Señor, and then we will talk about your daughter."

Felipe had handed the satchel to him and watched as he counted it. "Satisfied? It's all there. Now, where's Alejandra?"

The memories that resurfaced knocked him hard, and when Felipe came upon a rock formation he sat down on the ledge. Images played out as if it were all happening again. He leaned his elbows on his knees and held his face in his hands, willing the nightmare to end, but he could hear the little man chuckling and telling him to go to the end of his road, where it meets the highway. He'd gone there. He'd found Alejandra as the man had told him, but there was no life left in her. He sobbed at the memory. His little girl. He slumped forward, and let the tears come once again.

72.

BY SEVEN O'CLOCK, the parking lot was full of cars, and a sea of people flooded into the foyer. When it appeared the room could hold no more, Veronica Masters and Victor Ramirez stood on a riser behind the reception desk.

"Good evening, everyone, and welcome to Cala Luna," Victor began. "I am Victor Ramirez, and this resort is the realization of a dream I had several years ago. Now, a dream come true." He turned. "And when Veronica Masters shared one of her dreams with me, to mount an exhibition featuring the stunning work of an artist who lives in the area, I felt the same excitement I'd felt from my own dream. Please welcome Veronica Masters, who will tell you hers."

Veronica spoke briefly about her exhibition of my work in New York, and her dream to spend more time in Costa Rica, omitting our romantic liaison. She turned to me then. "I am proud to present artist Simon Patrick whose delightful work hangs before you tonight." Applause was enthusiastic so Veronica waited until it died down and she could be heard. "And this is the talented designer Sylvia Mendoza, from Nicaragua. The outfit I am wearing this evening is one of her creations." Sylvia smiled and curtsied. "She and my new friend, Marta, are both wearing Sylvia's creations and you will find other styles in her line on the upper mezzanine. Should you have any questions, we are all available to answer them. We hope you enjoy the exhibition."

As people milled around the paintings, I went up the stairs and stood on the mezzanine with Sylvia, a great vantage point. A little while later, Marco spotted us and climbed the stairs, first pausing in front of the triptych. Sylvia handed him a glass of wine. He smiled.

"Thank you, sweetheart. Congratulations, Simon."

"Thank you, but what for?"

"I saw a red dot on *Perilous Journey*."

"You're kidding. I don't believe it." I excused myself and went down the staircase, stopping at the triptych. I looked up at Marco and grinned, then continued down the stairs to the foyer, where people congratulated me on my work. I tried to answer their many questions.

Veronica found me and slipped her arm through mine, smiling proudly. "Are you starting to see dots in front of your eyes?" she whispered in my ear.

"I saw one."

"Try six." We strolled through the crowds gathered in front of my paintings, and I cast my eyes over them as we walked by, smiling into my wine glass when I spotted another red sticker.

"You're right. Incredible. Congratulations, Ms. V. I think you've got yourself a gallery in the making."

"I've had to explain to many of the buyers that the show will hang for two weeks, even though most of the paintings are sold. Some of them are from other countries, so we'll have to make adjustments. Victor is delighted. We're already planning our next show." She looked up at the mezzanine. "And women are slipping away to try on Sylvia's outfits in the washroom. She's doing well, too."

"Who bought *Perilous Journey*?" I whispered.

"Felipe Montoya. He wants to have dinner with us all before we leave." She kissed me on the cheek and said, "Going to do some more chatting. Catch you later."

I saw Marco standing alone in front of *Choice Location*, a painting of Don Verde perched on the pump handle. "You like

Don Verde, do you?" I asked when I walked up beside him. He jumped, coughed, and then turned to face me.

"Yes, I do, Simon. Very much. You've captured the essence of the bird. And that red dot signifies that I bought it." He smiled. Sincere.

"Well, thank you very much, Marco. It's funny, but I can't help remembering your reaction the first time you saw him when we joined you for lunch, when you got the migraine." But before Marco could respond, Veronica and Sylvia appeared on either side of us.

"Are our favourite gentlemen enjoying the evening?" Veronica asked, weaving her arm with Simon's.

I looked down at her and smiled, then glanced back at Marco before I replied. "Indeed, I am, and I think Marco would agree with me. Right, Marco?"

"Yes," Marco replied, putting his arm around Sylvia's shoulder. "It's a wonderful exhibition and I'm happy for all of you."

"So happy," I said, pointing to the red dot on *Choice Location*, "That he bought a painting of my buddy."

We mingled and schmoozed for what seemed an eternity. Sylvia looked radiant, buoyed by her obvious success. Veronica appeared relaxed and confident, yet I knew she was alert to any potential interest in my work. And me? I was extremely happy to shake the hands of so many satisfied patrons.

Later, when everyone had left but us, Victor suggested we join him for a celebratory drink. "Felipe and Marta are going to join us, too," Veronika said, tugging my arm.

The four of us joined Victor, his wife Leticia, Felipe, and Marta at a round mahogany table. Victor and Felipe rose from their chairs until we had seated the women. A waiter appeared with a bottle of champagne and four glasses for us. He poured our champagne, and before setting it in the ice bucket, removed an empty bottle that was already there, and secreted it away.

Victor raised his glass. "Let us drink to the success we've had today," he said. "To *our* success."

"To our success," we repeated.

More champagne flowed, chatter resumed, and Victor raised his glass again. "I propose a toast to the future and to more events like this one. To the future."

"To the future," we cheered in unison.

Veronica was the next to speak. "This show was magical; our guardian angel was with us all the way. We were shown that the climate is right for original art and fashion at Cala Luna. Victor and I have already been talking about another show before the end of the high season, perhaps after Easter. If that show goes as well as this one, Victor will give some serious thought to devoting room for a gallery and gift shop. I couldn't have hoped for anything better. Thank you, Victor." She turned to Sylvia and said, "From the beginning, your creations were also part of my dream. Thank you for making it a reality, Sylvia." She turned to me and smiled. "You, Simon Patrick, *gave* me the freedom to dream. When I saw your art, my first thought was to mount a show at my gallery in SoHo. Your art has proven itself in New York City and in Costa Rica. And now it's going to Mexico with Felipe and Marta, and, with other buyers, to Ireland, to Spain, and to the United States. Congratulations, Simon." More champagne arrived and we continued to talk until the wee hours when we all stumbled off to our quarters.

That night, we both fell asleep as soon as our heads hit the pillows.

73.

IT WAS DARK when the taxi dropped them off at Hotel Casablanca, a modest establishment across from the beach. They stashed the bag of money in the safe that was tucked into a wall in the closet, and Nick pocketed the key. He grabbed a couple of beers from their fridge and carried them out to the balcony. When Antonio finished in the bathroom, he joined him outside.

"Here's to another good day's work, bro," Nick said as he clinked Antonio's bottle. "I think that went well, don't you?"

"Well, since I don't have a clue about the going rates of gems, especially hot ones, and considering I have no other experience than our deal with Fat Tattooed Gerry in Bluefields, I'd say that twenty grand a piece is okay." He looked out over the water. "What do you think we should do next? How do you feel about going back to the house?"

"Well, it's already February," Nick said after consulting his watch. "We haven't heard anything, but then again, we haven't been into watching television or reading newspapers. Do you have anyone looking after the house while you're away?"

"Not really," Antonio said. "Unless Marco goes over. I could give him a call and see what's happening. He's the only person other than us who's got a key."

"Good idea to call him, but I'd buy another cellphone to call him, just in case anything has happened and they're on to us."

"I'll get one tomorrow."

When they'd finished their beers, they took turns in the shower, opened the safe, and peeled a few hundred off the wad in the bag. The casino was only a couple of blocks away and touted a restaurant that served imported North Atlantic lobster. They each ordered a Bloody Mary and sipped, awaiting their crustaceans.

"So how does it feel to be retired, Tony?" Nick crunched on the celery stick that garnished his drink. "From selling pencils when you were ten to being a millionaire before forty. Pretty sweet, bro. Better than my pension from the Marines."

"It hasn't sunk in yet, I guess," Antonio replied. The lobster had arrived, and he was preoccupied with cracking it open. When he'd pried a succulent piece from one of the claws and dipped it in garlic butter, he moaned ecstatically. He cleaned his palate with a sip of Bloody Mary and looked around the crowded dining room. "I've never *not* had to scheme, Nick. I don't know how I'll fill up my time. Maybe I'll buy a fleet of tourist launches, start a little business. Keep me honest. What about you?"

"Oh man, I'm just on the dole. This little haul will certainly keep me solvent for a while, if I'm careful. Who knows? Maybe I'll drive one of your boats."

They finished their lobsters, and when they'd paid their bill they went into the casino. The noise inside was akin to a football field full of winning pinball machines. Antonio made his way to the roulette wheel; Nick opted for the blackjack table. The tables weren't too far apart, so they had no problem seeing each other. Perhaps it was because they were the New Kids on the Block or simply Beginner's Luck, but they both won; it was same with their second bets, each of them raising the stakes—and winning. Antonio winked at Nick when he caught his eye. They continued a streak of winning that drew groans, heavy sighs, and hostile stares from losing opponents. When Antonio had won six turns in a row, he gathered the chips in front of him, thanked the players, and walked to the cashier.

While he was still waiting in line, Nick came up behind him with his handkerchief filled with chips.

"It seems we can do no wrong, bro." Nick cashed in and counted his earnings for the night while he waited for Antonio to finish with the cashier. "Came with three hundred, had a bitchin' lobster dinner, and I'm going home with nine hundred. Can't beat that."

"I think I can," said Antonio, fingering his bills. "I came with three as well, and I'm going home with twelve hundred." He grinned and wedged the money inside his wallet. "Let's get out of here before the house dicks jump on us."

They walked another block and were at the water. Waves crashed on the shore, and a sliver of moon shone clear and bright among starry constellations. Crickets, cicadas, and frogs thrummed in the warm night air. Both men were silent, perhaps reflecting on the evening's luck, or just letting the sounds of the night wash over them. The street lights illuminated the near distance, and in it, they saw a little woman bent over with the weight of bundles on her back. When they got closer, they saw that the woman had a pile of textiles on her back and a piece of fabric tied around her body, providing a sling for her sleeping baby. They were walking in the same direction, and when they caught up with her they towered over the diminutive Colombian woman. Her weathered face made her look like the grandmother of the baby she was carrying, but her bright eyes, her singsong voice, and her broad toothy smile spoke of her youth. She told them she had shawls for their wives, vests for themselves, blankets, and *mota*. At the mention of marijuana, Antonio and Nick both said yes in Spanish and English several times. The little woman put the bundles down on the sand and squatted next to them. She had hidden her little parcels of pot in-between two multicoloured, finely woven, wool blankets. She was selling *pulgares*, and true to their name, the little bundles were about the size of the end of an adult's thumb. Antonio said they'd take ten *pulgares* and she worked out the math and came up with one hundred U.S. dollars. Nick took out his wallet, Antonio took out his, and they gave the women one thousand instead. Both said thank you and patted her on the shoulder as they pocketed their purchases. She sat on the sand beside her bundles, clutched her baby with one arm, her other hand to her face, wiping tears away. "*Muchisima gracias, Señores. Que Dios los bendiga.*" They received her thanks and blessing and continued down the shoreline.

They hadn't walked much farther when two beautiful women appeared like apparitions drifting down the beach, their movements rhythmic, graceful, and fluid in their flowing cotton skirts. As they came closer, the two men stopped suddenly. "It's Rocío and Estrella," Nick said. "Holy shit." The women must have heard him. They were smiling.

"She said you would be here," Rocío said.

74.

IT APPEARED that everyone had slept late after the opening, and we all arrived at the dining room at the same time. Felipe, Marta, Marco, and Sylvia were just sitting down at the round table again, so we joined them.

"I trust everyone slept well?" I asked. Most people nodded and continued drinking their juices or doctoring their coffee.

Felipe sipped his coffee before he spoke. "I slept well, but I had the strangest dream. Our little girl was with a tiny woman with long, black hair. She was illuminated as if she had a halo. They were standing at the foot of our bed. I thought of the dream again this morning when I awoke and tried to rationalize what had inspired it." He sipped again before continuing. "Then I remembered that last night Veronica said that a guardian angel had been watching over you. That seemed sufficient justification. I was satisfied until Marta woke up, and I told her about it." He glanced at his wife, and she nodded. "I thought she was going to choke. She gasped when I told her. She had had the same dream." There was silence in the room, and I was the first to break it.

"Veronica and I saw the dark-haired woman at the foot of our bed, too. She was smiling and her arms were outstretched in a beatific posture, like statues of the Virgin Mary we've all seen," I told them. "It was a lovely dream vision, actually. And one I may paint." Marco coughed into his napkin. He looked at Sylvia, took her hand in both of his.

"It is no dream. The spirit of my deceased wife, Isabella, is visiting us," Marco explained. "She appeared to Sylvia and me at our home in Laguna de Apoyo some time ago. She has appeared to me before—when I am wide awake, but during those times, only I can see her. She died almost two years ago." He cleared his throat and drank some more coffee. "She seems to be my conscience. She makes subtle suggestions, and at times, I am sensitive enough to read into what she is showing me, to interpret." Marco poured more coffee from a carafe before he continued. "Isabella may indeed be our guardian angel, Veronica. She appears to approve of what we are all doing. She is radiant and smiling. It is a comforting visitation for me. I was brought up Catholic but never practised until after she died. I have been praying and lighting candles since then. I feel good about it, and if this is a result of it, I am truly grateful."

Marta looked at everyone and cleared her throat. "I have no problem believing this is true," she began. She wiped her eyes with her napkin and took a deep breath. "Each time I have become pregnant, the spirit of my mother visited me, to tell me when we had conceived even before doctors ever confirmed them. I welcomed her visits and felt very close to her spirit. And now, to see my baby girl with Isabella, I feel reassured. Like you, Marco, I am grateful whenever it happens, and I can honestly say that I welcome it."

The women were smiling, but all of them were gazing somewhere in the middle distance.

Veronica lifted her eyes and looked around the table. "I have Irish and Viking blood in my veins. But in circumstances like this, the Irish blood bubbles to the surface—the blood of my ancestors who believed in second sight, in spirits, and in faeries. Some of those beliefs I still hold dear. As a young girl, I was befriended by the spirit of my great-grandmother. My mother told me not to be so foolish when I first told her, so I never told her again. I grew to enjoy going to bed at night knowing that her spirit would be there with me." Veronica looked at me and smiled. “I must say, I was very comfortable with Isabella. And if I can speak for Simon, I think he was too.” I nodded. “And if she is, and continues to be, the guardian angel of us all, wherever we might be, we are truly blessed.” She leaned back in her chair with her coffee cup in her hands, sipping through the steam rising from it. When she set the cup back in the saucer, I took her hand and brought it to my lips. There were tears in her eyes.

75.

ANTONIO AND NICK were dumbstruck. They walked along the shore with Rocío and Estrella. Consolación had left them with the benediction, "God bless you," and it appeared that His blessings had been bestowed. Rocío walked beside Antonio and held his hand. Estrella linked her arm through Nick's and they walked together, speaking in low tones. They came upon some patio furniture outside a bar and sat down. A waiter came and took their order.

"So, girls," Nick started. "What brings you here to San Andrés?"

The twins both laughed at the same time. "You, Nick. You and Antonio," Rocío told them. "We followed you to Little Corn Island, too, but we just stayed in the background, watching. You gave the motor and gas and cooler full of beer to our cousins, Luís and Cristian." She smiled at her sister, then became serious. "A woman came to us the night you invited our family for dinner, when you gifted us. She stood in our room and told us to follow you, to take care of you."

Antonio and Nick looked at each other, and then asked simultaneously, "What woman? What did she look like? Did she tell you her name?"

They said she was tiny, and that she had long, black hair. They said she was beautiful. Radiant. It had to be Isabella, Antonio thought. Antonio knew that Nick didn't know what they were talking about. "Long story, Nick," he said. "I'll explain later."

They finished their drinks, paid the bill, and walked back to the hotel where they made themselves comfortable on chairs near the pool. Nick was asking Estrella questions about her father, Consolación.

"He was named after his great-grandfather, Consolación Flores, who was the personal slave of William Walker. When Walker ordered his men to burn down the city and was saddling up to leave, Flores told Walker he had forgotten a satchel and went back into the house. He opened the trap door and escaped through the tunnel under the house. The tunnel went straight to the lake. He swam to one of the islets, and when the dust and ashes settled, he caught a ride in a boat going to Little Corn Island." She looked at Nick and said, "Many of the people you talked with on Little Corn Island are our relatives."

They called Hector and told him that he was free to go back to Granada. Antonio had already given him a key to the house so that he could stay there and keep an eye on the place. They'd paid for a month in advance at Hotel Casablanca and were settling into the lazy rhythm of island life, enhanced by the delightful company of Rocío and Estrella. At some point, they would have to go back to Antonio's uncle's house to deal with the rest of the loot, but it was mostly gold bars, antique coins, and currency. They would investigate the coins on the internet when they returned to the island in Lake Nicaragua. In the meantime, they spent their days under water, in a world of multicoloured fish and pastel coral forests that undulated against the white sand, illuminated in the sunlight. They rented a catamaran and sailed to Providencia, a sister island in the San Andrés Archipelago. They left early in the morning and did some scuba diving until hunger drove them to a shoreline bar and restaurant. They ordered ceviche and sat in the shade of a *palapa* where the offshore breezes cooled them.

"That was some morning, bro," Nick drawled, sprawled in a double hammock with Estrella, sucking the lime wedge that had come with his Corona. "Such a silent, dreamy world. But deadly active."

"Truly beautiful, yet there are predators and prey, so there is also constant annihilation," Antonio mused. "I respect the ocean and know my place in it, which is out of the undertow and away from the jaws of a shark." Antonio gazed out over the water, silvered by the rays of the sun overhead. He cleared his throat, took a sip before he spoke. "I had a strange dream last night, and I wonder if it had something to do with Marco."

"How so?" Nick climbed out of the hammock and joined Antonio and Rocío at the table.

"Marco's wife, Isabella, appeared again," Antonio began. "She died a couple of years ago. Anyway, she didn't say anything, but her arms were spread wide, and she was smiling."

"That wasn't a dream, bro," Nick said. "We saw her too, didn't we, Estrella? I was wide awake. I had just closed my book and was turning off my reading lamp when she appeared at the foot of our bed. She looked just like you said, with her arms outstretched. And she was smiling. So what do you read into her appearance? What about Marco?"

"That she's forgiven Marco. Long story, but since I haven't been able to reach him, it could also be that she's his messenger, telling me he's alright." Antonio had bought another cellphone and had tried Marco's landline at the hacienda in Laguna de Apoyo, at their house on Lake Nicaragua, and his cell, all to no avail.

"This isn't the first time that I've been contacted through spirits and dreams," Antonio said. "Many people believe in their dreams, have since the beginning of time—they were revered for this ability and were sought for their advice. Technology is more revered now, a god to young and old." He wiped crumbs from his paper placemat and started folding it. "But if we can hold onto the old ways while embracing the new, we're doubly rewarded." He continued to fold the paper into an airplane. "Like my *abuela,*" he said. "She's always paid attention to her dreams and to her waking thoughts. She knew we were coming that day, Nick. She told me. And she can conjure up visitors by dwelling on them in her mind. But there she is with her cellphone. Comfortable in the spiritual world but also in cyberspace." He aimed the paper craft at a little boy playing in the sand. "*Abuela* can surf both worlds." Antonio chuckled. "It was because of her encouragement when I told her about a dream I had—that had later actually occurred—that I started paying attention to messages and dreams. Marco is alright. We don't need to worry about him."

76.

WE'D ALL FINISHED breakfast and were getting ready to leave the dining room. I had noticed Felipe on his cellphone. When he snapped it shut, he rose and asked for our attention.

"I've just received a call from the marina where my yacht is being repaired, and they tell me it is ready. Marta and I would like to invite you all to come with us on a cruise down the coast for a few days. There is more than enough room for everyone to sleep privately and comfortably. It would be an honour to have you all with us. I leave the invitation with you, and you can tell us later this morning what you have decided. We'll go and pack now." He bowed, and then put his arm around Marta. "Enjoy your morning."

We stood looking at each other. Sylvia and Veronica were grinning. Then we all started laughing like delighted children about to ride a roller coaster.

"What do you say, Marco?" I asked. "Can you spare the time?"

Marco looked at Sylvia, who was still grinning. "From the look on Sylvia's face I think the answer is yes." Marco put his arm around her. "I don't know if I can live up to a real honeymoon after this fantastic rehearsal." He kissed her. "And what about you two?"

Veronica had threaded her arm through mine. "I don't have any commitments. This show was a hit. Why not?"

The word "yacht" to me meant a large cruiser, but what we saw at the marina was a ship that took up several slips and made the other boats look like toys in a bathtub. It rose so high on the water that we had to climb a gangway that had been lowered from the top deck. I think Felipe said it was sixty-feet long. There were two decks below the bridge. While Felipe owned the vessel, it was the captain who gave the orders to his crew, the two men who had doubled as bodyguards at Cala Luna. He had a staff to cook and serve our meals as well as clean our cabins, which were spacious. It was a relaxed environment with sufficient space so that no one felt crowded. On the top deck was a small swimming pool with lounge chairs in an area shaded with canvas.

On our first evening, as we sat and sipped after-dinner brandies, Felipe referred to Marco's valiant rescue of his son, Alfonso.

Marco looked a bit embarrassed and tried to change the topic of conversation. "That's very kind of you, Felipe." He leaned back and sipped his drink. "Very kind to take us to dinner." Felipe brushed his statement away and smiled, but Marco continued. "That evening, you told me that you brought bodyguards with you because people wanted to 'eliminate' you. That your daughter had been kidnapped. Why would that be, Felipe?"

Felipe cleared his throat and also leaned back in his chair. "I'm sure you all know about Mexico's problems: corruption, the proliferation and power of drug cartels," he said, looking around.

We nodded our awareness, listening intently.

"My property appeals to them, to grow their crops. A couple of years ago, I was approached by one of their 'negotiators' to work out a deal for the land." Felipe swirled his cognac, sipped. "I told him I was not interested. But that was not the answer they wanted. We were threatened. And then they kidnapped my daughter and killed her." He grimaced and looked at his wife. He sighed and shook his head. "So we decided to go away for a while before we all disappeared against our will."

Marco nodded. "But are you not concerned about your property while you are away?"

Felipe smiled, opened his mouth, and it appeared he was about to respond when the lights went out. From the galley, flaming desserts were paraded in, to blaring canned mariachi trumpets. Conversation stopped, and all eyes were fixed on the Baked Alaska in front of us.

The three women had formed some kind of sisterhood and spent a lot of time together, laughing and chatting. I guessed we men had a similar "hood," but it was intermittent, with long silent spaces in-between. It wasn't as if we were avoiding each other, but we also didn't seek each other out to converse. We often all found ourselves in or around the pool, relaxing, and the company was pleasant as we slowly broiled under a tropical sun.

Despite the amount of sunscreen I slathered on Veronica, her freckles were closing in on her. Soon, they would all be seamlessly connected, and her skin would morph to a new shade: a caramel or butterscotch blue-eyed Irish Viking. She loved it, and so did I. In fact, I loved being at sea. The abundance of marine life was incredible and inspiring. Pods of whales breached just beyond us; dolphins frolicked around the ship, diving under us and bobbing up on the other side. Veronica spotted a leatherback turtle and flying fish. I soaked in the images, taking the odd photograph, but mostly absorbing everything around me.

One evening, after dinner, Veronica went to our cabin to get a shawl and said she'd join me on the top deck. When I got there, Marco was leaning on the railing. I joined him and stood beside him. Marco nodded to me and continued looking out to sea. We were at anchor about two miles out off the coast of the Nicoya Peninsula. It was dark, with only a sliver of new moon. He pointed into the water. "See the sparkling lights in the waves? Amazing. I've been swimming in the moonlight with these lights all around me. It's plankton, and the motion disturbs them, causing them to emit those lights. It's called bioluminescence. Incredible, isn't it?"

"It is," I replied. "I remember you saying you used to surf in the water off where the Cala Luna is now located. Are you from Costa Rica originally?"

"Yes, I'm Tico. I was born and raised in San José. I just moved to Nicaragua a couple of years ago." He continued to stare dreamily at the water.

"You didn't happen to live at Tamarindo, did you?" I continued to lean on the railing. We were both still facing the water. Marco turned. We faced each other. "That's how you know Don Verde, isn't it?"

"Yes, Simon, you're right. I did live there with Isabella." He felt for cigarettes he didn't have; instead, he inhaled and exhaled deeply before he continued. "I went to Nicaragua to start over."

"Well, it looks like you've succeeded," I said, thinking of all the pieces of the puzzle that were finally fitting into place. "And by the appearance to us all of a smiling Isabella, she appears to approve of what you are doing."

"And what are you going to do, now that you know, Simon?" Marco asked.

"I don't think I'm going to do anything, Marco. You are supporting a home for abused women. That certainly goes in your favour. You saved Felipe's son from being washed away in a riptide. You're a good person, Marco. But from what Don Verde has told me, I gather you used him for delivering merchandise to freighters. I met one of your customers, I think. He came in on a dinghy." We both heard laughter; Veronica and Sylvia were approaching. "Maybe we can talk later."

After breakfast the next morning, the women were lingering over their coffee, animated in conversation, so I decided to get some exercise. I started walking around the deck. Marco was already walking, so I joined him. We walked in silence for a couple of laps. Then Marco asked, "How do you like living in Tamarindo, Simon?"

"I love it," I said. "I am inspired there, as you've seen from the work I've been doing." We continued walking.

Marco looked off in the distance, then at me. He pointed to a row of deck chairs, and we sat down. "I am glad that you're happy there. It's a good place. Someone needs to enjoy it. Have you heard anything further of the investigation?" His leg jiggled, but he didn't seem to notice.

"I haven't heard anything since the detectives were at the house. They haven't been back, and I haven't read anything in *La Nación*. I imagine it's a cold case. They interviewed Don Verde though." I chuckled. Marco didn't. "He's a talkative fellow," I added. "He speaks English now and talks just like me."

"That's a relief." Both legs were going now.

"Look Marco, I realize you're a good guy."

Marco looked up and down the deck and then leaned towards me. "Please believe me when I say that I didn't kill Isabella," he said in one breath. "We fought and she hit me on the head with a vase that had been filled with water. When I went toward her, she slipped and hit her head on the corner of the desk." He sighed and rested against the back of the deck chair. "I am guilty, though, of putting her in the well. I was so afraid and didn't know what to do." He shut his eyes. When he opened them again he said, "Please believe me."

"I believe you, Marco," I said. I put my hand on his shoulder. "We all have history, baggage, whatever. I believe you. It was a tragic accident, and a complicated one."

"What was so complicated, gentlemen?" Veronica and Sylvia appeared beside us. They were in high spirits, so they must not have heard the rest of our conversation.

77.

WHEN HECTOR SPLASHED down near the dock and drifted in, it was already late afternoon. The lake was quiet save for the lapping of the water agai nst the rocks and a light breeze that had been his tailwind. He secured the plane, unloaded his gear, and lugged it up to the door.

The place looked alright, he thought. There were some empty beer bottles on the counter, a half a dozen cold ones left among the condiments in the fridge. He was glad he'd stopped at a supermarket to get a few things. He might try to catch something but didn't want to go hungry if the fish didn't bite. He opened a beer and went outside to light the barbecue. While he waited for the coals to burn, he wandered through the house, checking the rooms. One bed was rumpled, but all the rest were neat and in order. He called Antonio from the landline.

"Hey Antonio," he said. "I'm here at the house. Everything looks okay. There were a bunch of beer bottles on the counter and one of the beds has been slept in, but other than that, it's clean and neat."

"Marco was probably there for a while."

"Probably," Hector agreed. "Whoever it was had a key. No sign of forced entry. Everything is tight."

"Good to hear, Hector. Stay as long as you want, but give me a call when you are planning to leave."

"Thanks, Antonio. I have a flight to Léon in a couple of

days, but I'll let you know if something else comes up. Talk to you soon."

Hector took his steak out of the fridge, studded it with slivers of garlic, and set it on the grill. He sat in a lounge chair by the pool while it cooked. The sun was setting, and in the dim light he watched a quetzal fly into the branches of the Ceiba that towered above him. A strong cooling breeze blew from the east. He leaned back and closed his eyes, and moments later he was dozing. A hand touched his shoulder, and he awoke with a start. He looked up to see a beautiful woman smiling at him and pointing in the direction of the barbecue. He ran to it and pulled the steak off; lucky for him, he liked his meat well done. He looked back to the chair where he'd been sitting. The woman was gone.

After dinner, he lay on the sofa in the living room and turned on the television. He found an old Western starring John Wayne. It was in English with subtitles, and though he loved Westerns, his eyes were too tired to pay attention. He turned it off and went to bed. There were magazines and a couple of paperbacks on the bedside table, but he turned out the light and lay back.

The same beautiful woman appeared at the foot of his bed, illuminated, like her entire tiny body had a halo around it. She was smiling. She came to sit on the bed. She smoothed the bedcovers; her fingers touched his leg. "Tell Antonio not to worry," she said softly. "He can come home." She patted the bed once again and disappeared.

Hector abruptly sat up and turned on the light. Everything was as he remembered it except that she was gone. He looked at his cellphone; it was only ten o'clock. He went to the kitchen and picked up the landline. "Antonio, it's me, Hector."

"What's up, Hector? Everything alright?"

"I think so. But I've had a visitor. A woman."

"How did she get there? Are you having a good time? And if you are, why are you calling me?"

"She's gone. At least for now. She's a ghost, Antonio. A friendly spirit. She told me to tell you not to worry. That it's alright for you to come home."

"Isabella," Antonio said and then, distracted, hung up.

78.

WE HAD GONE as far south as Quepos and Playa Manuel Antonio on the coast and we were nearing the end of our voyage. We moored offshore, spent the night, and in the morning took the motorboat in to the white sands of the national park. As we walked along the shore, howler monkeys hooted at us. Further up from the water, a group of people had gathered in a circle and were looking down at the sand.

"Jaguar tracks, folks," a rotund man in a straw hat and a gaudy shirt drawled in a Texan accent. "Must have come by earlier this morning. Keep an eye out." We murmured that we would and continued on to a restaurant Felipe recommended.

Everyone was totally relaxed, tanned, and happy. At dinner, on the night before we were to sail back to Playa Langosta, Felipe had his chef prepare a feast of seafood that outshone all the other great meals he had made us. We'd dressed for dinner and were having liqueurs and coffee, sated from the meal and the several bottles of wine we'd consumed. Everyone was jolly except for Marco, who appeared distracted. He looked around and cleared his throat.

"I feel I must make a confession to you all, since you have been so kind, generous, and hospitable." Marco took another sip of his liqueur, then his coffee, as he gathered his thoughts before he continued. "You have all seen the spirit of Isabella. And it is she whom I must tell you about. Simon knows parts of this story but not entirely. Nor does my lovely fiancée, Sylvia.

The coincidence of our meeting is incredible. Simon owns the house I fled when my wife, Isabella, died. The subject of several of his paintings happens to be a parrot I owned and trained to smuggle drugs to freighters anchored offshore." Marco looked around the room, pausing to make eye contact with Felipe. "I might add that I retired some time ago."

When they went to their stateroom that night, Marco felt anxious. He sat on the edge of the bed where Sylvia was taking off her sandals. "I feel I must tell you the entire story of my life at Playa Tamarindo," he said. He took both her hands in his. "I've showed you my scars and you've shown me yours. We both know lives of arguments and abuse, abuse that was physical as well as emotional. Isabella and I often argued and the arguments escalated to out-and-out physical fights.

"The day she died, we had been fighting. She threw a vase at me that hit my head. I fell, and when I lunged at her, she slipped. The fall cracked her skull. She died from it, and I was so frightened, I hid her body in our well. Simon found her some months later, after he'd purchased the house, and an investigation ensued. I fled to Nicaragua, and you know the rest." His eyes were brimming with tears. "I hope that you will forgive me, Sylvia. I would never do anything to hurt you. I was so filled with remorse from what I had done, what I was running from, that I tried to make up for it. That is why I bought the house at Laguna de Apoyo."

"I appreciate your honesty, Marco," she said. Tears were in her eyes and in her voice. "You shocked me with this confession, but I believe you and I know you are a good person." She stood and put her hands on his shoulders. "We have all seen Isabella. She is with us, and I think she approves of what we are doing. If not, she would haunt us and make our lives miserable. But it has been the opposite—for all of us. When she appears, it is like she is blessing us. I often wondered who you lit candles for each morning, but now I understand. I do forgive you, Marco. It was tragic, but it was an accident, one you can't confess to the authorities, but I am grateful you told me and I do forgive you. And I think Isabella does too."

He stood and circled his arms around her. "And when we get back and unpack, we can think about going to San Andrés." Sylvia smiled and nodded. They kissed and tumbled onto the bed. A soft and salty breeze from the ocean wafted in from their open window and caressed their limbs as they slept.

79.

"HEY, HECTOR, how's it going?" Antonio put the cellphone closer to his ear. "Yeah, we've got one week left here. Can you meet us at the airport here in San Andrés a week from today? Great. Oh, yeah, Hector, you'll be taking back two more passengers. See you soon, man." He clapped his phone shut. "Says he'll take us all back to my uncle's place." They were having lunch at a sidewalk restaurant, reminiscing about the month they'd spent there, when Marco and Sylvia walked by holding hands.

"Hey, Marco!" Antonio called to him. Marco turned around and saw the group seated at a table. "Come and join us." Nick rose to move two more chairs to their table. Antonio introduced Sylvia and Marco to everyone.

"What are you guys doing here?" Marco asked.

"We could ask you the same thing," Antonio said, and motioned for the waiter to come and serve them.

"We've just gotten back from a brief cruise with some new friends," Marco replied.

Antonio grinned, then ordered a round of beer for everyone. "We've been here for a month, hanging out, scuba diving, relaxing," he said.

"Hiding out would be more appropriate, wouldn't it?" Marco quipped, his eyebrows slightly raised.

"Whatever you think. The offshore breezes are so pleasant here, and it was getting hot in Granada."

Marco sipped his beer. "In more ways than one, I bet," he smirked.

Sylvia kept quiet but looked questioningly at Marco who mouthed that he would tell her later.

"But we're heading back next week," Antonio said. "Hector is flying in to collect us. He's been staying at the house and says that everything is cool." He leaned over to Marco. "Isabella visited him and told him it was safe for us to come back."

"You too?" Marco smiled, and squeezed Sylvia's hand, who simply nodded.

80.

SYLVIA AND MARCO had booked into a hotel down the road from Antonio and Nick. They spent some time together—evenings, mostly, but kept to themselves otherwise. They rented bicycles and toured the island, exploring the caves that were rumoured to hold Captain Morgan's buried treasure.

On the day Antonio, Nick, Rosío, and Estrella were to leave, they all took a launch to Johnny Cay to have lunch and spend the afternoon before Hector arrived. Sylvia got along well with Rosío and Estrella, and they went swimming together while the men sat beneath a *palapa*. At four o'clock, they took a boat back to San Andrés, changed their clothes, and when they arrived in the lobby a half hour later, they saw Hector climb out of a taxi outside their hotel. He had a newspaper tucked under his arm. They all walked across the street to a bar and, once seated, Antonio ordered beer for everyone.

"Good to see you again, Hector. Everything alright on the home front?"

"Everything's fine. Thought you might like to see this morning's newspaper."

Antonio opened the newspaper Hector handed him and saw the article to which he referred.

Robbery Suspect Found Dead

The sole suspect in the bombing and robbery at Banco LAFISE Bancentro was found dead yesterday morning. The body of César

> Sanchez was found floating near the pier at the foot of Calle La Calzada. His blood-alcohol level was 2.0. No foul play is suspected.
>
> Sanchez was believed to have opened a tunnel beneath a house that he rented on Calle El Arsenal and extended it westward to Banco LAFISE Bancentro where he planted a bomb to open the wall near the safety deposit boxes on December 24.
>
> After extensive interviews with its customers, Banco LAFISE Bancentro estimates that more than two million dollars' worth of money, gold, and jewellery was stolen. But curiously, all the wills, deeds, and documents stored in the safety deposit boxes were recently returned by mail.

Antonio looked up from the newspaper and grinned at Nick. "Well, what do you know, Nick? I think Isabella is still with us. It's almost unbelievable, but a man named César Sanchez drowned in Lake Nicaragua."

"We are lucky, bro," Nick said and grinned.

"The envelope that's mentioned, that was the envelope that I put in the mail, wasn't it?" Hector said. "The ghost was telling me that it was safe for you to go back to your house for that reason. Am I right?"

"You're right, Hector, and the people you introduced us to have been the recipients of our spoils. You too, actually," Antonio said. He motioned for another round.

"You guys are too much," Hector said, then snorted. "You should make a movie."

81.

IN A FEW SHORT YEARS, my little corner of the world has become the hub from which my art travels the globe. The Lasting Image Gallery now has a satellite gallery at the Cala Luna Resort where I have two exhibitions a year and two at Veronica's flagship gallery in New York. The Four Seasons Resort never panned out. Gerardo Lopez had probably heard of Cala Luna's success, so the partners had backed down.

Veronica comes here several times a year; she is selling Sylvia's creations and has discovered two young Costa Rican artists that she is promoting in both galleries with a New York exhibition lined up for them next year. Felipe and Marta have connections with a gallery in Mexico City where I periodically ship canvases and, in turn, they occasionally transfer money to my bank account. Felipe is talking with the curator of a nature museum in Mexico City. He wants to donate *Perilous Journey*, with the proviso that they enhance their exhibition of endangered species, including the plight of leatherback turtles. It seems their gratitude to Marco—or to Isabella—was doubly magnified when they returned to their farm and learned that boys from the opium cartel that targeted Felipe's family had tried, unsuccessfully, to set fire to the place. They'd fled, leaving their gas cans on the perimeter of the property as well as a pair of soiled trousers. Since then, Felipe's workers overheard people talking in Oaxaca City, saying that they were working on a farm that was cursed. But Felipe felt blessed.

In April, Don Verde brought home his own *novia,* Esmeralda. Their courting inspired a few of my newest canvases, and when she nested and hatched a chick, the entire family became the subject of a series. Don Verde and Esmeralda are attentive parents. When the fledgling was ready to take flight, the three of them painted the sky. The image was immortalized on canvas and remains deeply etched in my memory. Of course, they continue to live and talk in our environment—constant lime green flashes. Esmeralda says the odd word, but she mostly defers to Don Verde. But while he has a mate that keeps him occupied, Don Verde is still a rascal that maintains his perch on my easel, shouting out phrases in English and Spanish that echo everyone around here.

We attended Sylvia and Marco's wedding at Laguna de Apoyo in May, and we've just heard that Sylvia is pregnant. They have asked us to be godparents. We met Antonio and Rocío at the wedding, and her identical twin, Estrella, was with Nick. They announced an imminent double wedding. Veronica and I? We're committed to each other and our delightfully schizophrenic comings and goings. It seems we enjoy the best of both worlds, so why change anything?

I've been working on the image of Isabella as she appeared to us at the foot of our bed and just finished it this morning. For some reason, it has taken me longer than any other painting. I felt shy for some reason. I felt like I was being watched. But when I woke up this morning, whatever trepidation I had vanished.

82.

ALEXANDRA HELD ISABELLA'S HAND as they floated through acres of opium blossoms. It was the day before the workers would arrive to harvest—backbreaking work for abhorrent wages. Together, Alexandra and Isabella lifted their hands to the heavens. The sun was high in the sky and fluffy clouds, like tufts of cotton, drifted in the breeze. The clouds moved, slowly at first, then gathered momentum, as they held their hands up in supplication. Lightning flashed, crackling across the sky. The wind came up and the clouds darkened, thunder rumbling deep within them. Isabella pointed to a stand of trees, and in an instant, lightning struck the trees, igniting them like kindling. Alexandra looked at Isabella and smiled. The little spirit wiggled her fingers over the fields of poppies, and they too, ignited.

A watchman saw the trees on fire and roared into the field on his ATV. As more of the field caught fire, he took out his cellphone to make a call. When the person he was calling answered, a whirlwind of embers and ashes whipped around the watchman. He dropped the phone just before he was whisked away, hurtled head over heels through the smoky fields by an unseen force.

Isabella caressed Alexandra's head and smiled down at her. "Our work here is now done, Little One."

Acknowledgements

I am grateful for friends and acquaintances in Granada, Nicaragua, in Costa Rica, and in Canada. Thank you, Leonardo Valasquez, my friend and dentist in Granada, who with his friend, Rafael Martinez, a William Walker aficionado, showed me where Walker lived and one of his offices, as well as recounted legends of the tyrant's time in Granada.

In Jacó, Costa Rica, my thanks to Luís Fonseca, biologist and founder of Neo-Fauna, a rescue preserve for birds, animals, and reptiles. He taught me about my character, Don Verde, his scientific name, *Amazona auropaliata,* and that parrots are truly individuals with different behaviours and markings, which distinguish one from another.

In the early stages, many kind and patient friends read various drafts of *What Goes Around;* they asked questions, made comments, and encouraged me. Thanks to Alma, Brenda, Cindy, Craig, Janine, Jean, Kathi, Lee, Marietta, Mary, Shannon, and Ursula. And the greatest thanks of all to my loving husband, Rick Beaver, who takes good care of me.

In the next important stage of creating the book, my thanks to Luciana Ricciutelli, editor extraordinaire, whose careful eyes, thorough vetting, and creative suggestions were all so welcome in the process of making the book better. Thank you also to